TALON VENGEANCE

TALON
BOOK 3

BRENT TOWNS

ROUGH
EDGES
PRESS

Talon Vengeance
Paperback Edition
Copyright © 2023 Brent Towns

Rough Edges Press
An Imprint of Wolfpack Publishing
9850 S. Maryland Parkway, Suite A-5 #323
Las Vegas, Nevada 89183

roughedgespress.com

Paperback ISBN 978-1-68549-219-9
eBook ISBN 978-1-68549-218-2
LCCN 2022949512

TALON VENGEANCE

PREVIOUSLY...

"YOU ARE BACK," Leonid said as he watched Anja enter the room. "Tell me, how did things go?"

She stared at him. "Give me another name."

He held up a hand, the chain from the cuffs rattling on the tabletop. "Wait, wait. I want something from you first. Did you get the girl?"

"Yes."

He stared at her. "Judging by the expression on your face I'd say it wasn't easy. I'd say you lost someone."

Anja shrugged her shoulders. The last thing she wanted to do was play games with this animal.

Leonid smiled expectantly. "It wasn't Jake, was it? Tell me it was him."

"No."

"But you did lose someone."

"So did Section Three."

"Oh, dear. They are very good at what they do. Which means you and your people are better. Maybe you are ready for this next one."

Anja leaned across the table forcing the Russian to sit back. "Give me a fucking name," she growled savagely.

"Oh, you're going to love this one. Wolfgang Hermann."

"The German minister?"

Leonid's eyes lit up. "The one and only."

"But how?"

"By keeping it out of Germany. He hires people to do all the work for him."

"Where?"

"Belgrade. That's where he peddles his specialty."

"And what does he specialize in?" Anja asked.

"African girls. He's like a modern-day slaver."

"Tell me more."

Leonid smiled. "You're going to have to go to Tanzania."

CHAPTER ONE

Dodoma, Tanzania, 3 Days Later

"BLOODY HELL, there is always some tosser trying to shoot me!" Jacob Hawk exclaimed as he swung hard on the steering wheel of a battered gray Land Rover. Bullets punched into the vehicle's thin skin as the shooters in the three vehicles following opened fire once more.

"At least you didn't steal an expensive ride this time, Jake," came the calm voice of Anja Meyer, the team's commander, over the comms.

"Only because there bloody wasn't one to flog," he shot back at her as he hit a pothole and the vehicle bounced and shuddered violently, wrenching the wheel in his hands.

The former SAS operator ground the gears of the Land Rover as he tried to bleed another ounce of speed out of the tired beast. "Fuck me, what a piece of shit."

He worked the clutch, and his knee came up and hit the steering wheel. Being six foot four had its advantages but was a drawback in a situation such as this. Sweat ran down the whiskers of his unshaven face, cutting tracks in the coating of dust coming through the open window. "Can we at least get the intel right on the next op?"

"It was done on the fly, Jake," Ilse Geller responded. "You knew there would be risks involved."

He mumbled something incoherent as the Land Rover began another lap of the large roundabout.

"Say again, Bravo One?" Ilse said, using his callsign.

"I said, Roger that."

"Whatever you do, Jake, don't lose the package," Anja said to him.

Hawk glanced briefly over his shoulder before bringing his eyes back to the road. He'd caught a glimpse of the man lying in the back of the vehicle; his mouth was taped shut, his eyes were open, and his chest covered in blood from a bullet exit wound. "Oops."

"Say again, Bravo."

"Just talking to myself," he replied as he swung hard once more on the steering wheel and pointed the nose of the vehicle through the center of the roundabout towards a bridge spanning a narrow creek that ran through the city.

The next voice Hawk heard was that of Karl Wolff, the team's OCD tech who'd once been a field agent for MI6 where he'd been captured and tortured. "Bravo One, there is a roadblock on the bridge. You can't go that way."

Hawk's foot pressed harder on the gas pedal.

"Acknowledge, Bravo One."

Hawk started moving in the driver's seat as he tried to urge the vehicle to go faster. Tiredly, the needle on the speedometer started to climb a little higher, while behind it more gunfire stung the vehicle's exterior savagely.

"Jake, what are you doing?" Karl asked.

Higher still the needle climbed.

"Damn it, Jake, what the hell are you doing?"

"When I was growing up, I used to watch a show on

TV that I liked a lot. It was called *The Dukes of Hazard*. Ever heard of it?"

"No."

"Then hang on, Karl, you're going to enjoy this."

———

ILSE'S brown eyes widened as her anxiety rose exponentially. "Oh, shit!"

Standing beside her was Anja Meyer. Thin, short blonde hair, dressed in jeans and a T-shirt, mid-thirties. Ilse, on the other hand, had mousy colored hair and fine features. An athletic build, she was the team's intelligence officer. A role she had once held whilst she worked with Anja for German intelligence.

"What is it?" Anja asked.

"He's going to jump the vehicle across the creek," she said urgently.

Anxiously, the pair watched the feed coming through on the large screen before them. A sudden explosion erupted from close by the Land Rover and it seemed to waver on the road.

"Jake, are you alright?" Ilse asked.

"Where the hell did these cocks get rocket launchers from?" he growled.

"Ilse, see if you can get a close up shot of one of those vehicles," Anja said.

The aerial view came in closer, showing nothing. "Jake, go around again," Ilse said.

"What?"

"I'm trying to get a look at who it is that's chasing you."

"You've got to be shitting me."

"Come on, Jake, it's not like it's a small roundabout. Even I can see from here it's at least two-hundred meters across. You can play your boy's game and kill yourself later."

"Ah, bollocks," Hawk growled. "You people have no faith."

Both women were relieved to see Hawk's ride veer violently left, its rear end sliding sideways. The three vehicles followed him, and the ISR feed was able to get a better look at a couple of occupants. "They're white," Anja said.

"Yes," Ilse replied. "Hired thugs? Karl, see what you can do with that frame."

"Could be."

Ilse's eyes widened a touch when she saw a long tubular object appear from the lead vehicle. She recognized it instantly. "Jake, RPG!"

The explosion behind the Land Rover erupted skyward, a cloud of dirt and dust covering the vehicle.

For a moment they held their breath before the Land Rover exploded from the other side.

"I hope you got what you needed because I'm out of here," Hawk shouted over the comms.

"Where, Jake? Where are you going to go?"

"Across the creek."

Anja put a palm up to her forehead. "Fuck me."

Ilse glanced at her; the profanity falling from her commander's mouth was somewhat unusual. "What?" Anja asked, looking back at Ilse. "He's frigging crazy."

She touched her transmit button. "You hear that, Jake. You're fucking crazy."

"My most memorable trait."

"What about the package, Jake?"

"The package is kaput."

"Say again, Bravo?" Anja's voice suddenly held a hard edge to it.

"He's screwed. Got shot a while back. Didn't have the heart to tell you."

"Fuck!" The headset went flying across the room. She whirled on Ilse. "You tell him that he'd better hope that these bastards kill him because if they don't, I will."

"Oh, I think he'll do that to himself," Ilse said as she watched him careen towards the creek.

———

"DON'T FUCK THIS UP, JAKE," Hawk said to himself.

Once more he straightened the Land Rover up and pointed it towards the bridge. The battered vehicle had acquired several more rattles in the past few minutes and the speed suddenly reduced.

The creek bank appeared in front of him and at that moment Hawk realized it was not one of his better judgment calls. "Oh, bollocks!"

The bank had a small uplift point which acted as a rough ramp. The front of the Land Rover came up and met thin air. The forces of gravity cut in, and the battered vehicle plunged down the embankment and into the shallow water, stopping instantly. The Talon field agent slammed into the steering wheel, the breath leaving his body with an audible whoosh.

Pain ripped through him, and for a moment Hawk thought he'd broken something. He let out a low groan and heard Ilse say, "You're an idiot, Jake."

"Yeah, well, it worked for the Duke boys. Shit."

He glanced in the back once more to see that the corpse had slid onto the floor. "Got to go, Armin."

Armin Wagner had been the target of the mission to Tanzania. According to Leonid Federov, Wagner was high up in Wolfgang Hermann's Tanzanian operation, Hermann being the current Minister of Defense in the German government. The plan had been to capture Wagner, extract as much information as they could from him, dismantle the Tanzanian end, and try to bring Hermann out of his comfort zone before nailing him to the wall. Thus, inflicting more pain on the global human trafficking market of Medusa. The intention was that with another buyer out of the way, they were that one step closer to shutting Medusa, and their new CEO Ilya Noskov, down. It was like dismantling a house one brick at a time. It may not look to be much, but if you take enough away, then the whole structure will come crashing down.

Bullets peppered the Land Rover as Hawk slipped out the door. The glass in it shattered and the Talon operator felt the displacement of air as a couple of rounds passed close by his face.

He hunkered down and retrieved his Glock from the waistband of his pants where he'd tucked it. He rose, steadied himself, and then blew off four shots, hitting one shooter and forcing the other to take cover.

Hawk suddenly abandoned the cover provided by the Land Rover and ran along the creek bank. From the roadblock on the far end of the bridge, more shots rang out. Bullets thudded into the ground around him as he used some brush for cover.

"Bravo, sitrep, over." It was Ilse.

"Just pretending I'm Linford Christie, Alpha Two. Think I might—"

WHACK!

"Shit, that was close."

"Are you alright?"

"For the moment. Where is the big man and his team?"

"Ten mikes out," Ilse replied.

"How the fuck can he still be ten out?" Hawk snarled into his comms as he ran. "He was ten out ten minutes ago when shit started to go south."

"That was your call, Jake, remember? You wanted to

do it—what did you say—like Robinson Crusoe because you didn't want the target spooked."

Bullets sliced through the bushes along the creek bank. "Do you know who these bastards are?"

"Karl is working on it."

"Work faster—" He ducked as another bullet passed close. "We need to know who they are."

A large boulder lay ahead of him on the creek bank and Hawk slid to a stop behind it. He peered around just as a shooter crashed through the bushes before him. "Careless, cock," he grated and put two rounds in the man's chest.

The man was wearing body armor but still fell from the hammer blows. Hawk waited for him to stop his short slide before shooting him again. There was no coming back from a hole in the head.

He quickly bent down and took the man's weapon. It was a Heckler and Koch G36K. He checked it over briefly before stooping to take several spare magazines from the shooter's webbing.

Before Hawk straightened up, he went through the dead man's pockets. Finding nothing, he decided to check the man's arms for identifying marks. The guy was Caucasian, maybe European and—

"Got you," Hawk said as he looked at the tattoo on the man's arm. He glanced up as he dug out his cell, took a quick picture and put it away—just in time, as two shooters appeared through the brush.

The G36 came up and he depressed the trigger, bullets from the magazine spraying them. They tumbled to the ground in a tangle of arms and legs, and he added one to each man's head for good measure.

Not waiting for reinforcements to appear, he climbed the bank and broke clear of the brush. Pausing momentarily, he glanced along the dirt street. The creek acted as a kind of barrier between the civilized part of the city and the rest.

Across from him were some rundown compounds. He glanced to his right and then ran.

He made it halfway. It was then that three motorbike riders appeared. Trailbikes, suitable for the terrain and the conditions. "You've got to be fucking kidding."

Hawk stopped and brought the G36 up and fired at the first rider. The man jerked under the impact of the 5.56 rounds before falling from his bike. The machine lay over on its side and skidded towards the Talon operator, stopping just short.

The two remaining riders produce MP7s which were hanging from straps draped over their shoulders.

Hawk shook his head. "Who the fuck are these guys?"

It might look good for movies but shooting one-handed from a moving motorbike was just stupid. But spraying enough ammunition around might score you a lucky shot.

The Talon agent went down onto his belly as bullets kicked up around him. The two bikes roared past, and their brake lights came on as they slowed.

Hawk came to his feet and brought the G36 up. He depressed the trigger and the first of the two riders toppled to the ground. He shifted his aim, and another burst achieved the same result.

Sudden shouts from the creekbank drew his attention and he saw more shooters appear. "Alpha Two, I need an exfil, now."

He fired once more but the stream of bullets turned to a trickle then nothing as the magazine ran dry. For a moment he was seized by anguish, and he cursed himself for not doing a tactical reload. But the two shooters he'd spotted had dropped down behind the bank out of sight as they took cover.

This gave Hawk the chance he needed. He turned and ran towards the mudbrick wall opposite which fenced the nearest compound. And as a renewed burst of bullets peppered everything around him, he leaped over the fence.

———

"WHAT DO WE HAVE?" Anja asked.

"At the moment, we've got X-Rays after him from the vehicles along with the ones from the bridge," Ilse replied.

"Where did the ones on the bikes come from?"

"No idea."

"These people are too well organized just to be ordinary shooters. Someone is backing them. We need to get Jake out of there now before he winds up dead."

"I'm working on finding him a route."

"See if you can vector him towards Mr. Harvey and his men."

"That might be a bit hard at the moment. There are more men coming in from that direction."

"Shit, that's all we need. Do what you can but get him out of there."

"Yes, ma'am." She paused. "Jake, I need you to go southeast across the railway line. You have about 200 meters ahead of you to make it."

"Roger that."

"I've got a helicopter in the air approaching from the north," Karl said. "Looks to be an NH90."

Anja started to look worried. "Damn it, Karl, find out where they're coming from. This mess is just getting larger the longer it goes on. We've kicked the hornets' nest, but I want to know who the fucking lead hornet is."

"Surely they have to be tied to Hermann," Ilse suggested.

"That would make sense, but there is so much to this operation. Well-equipped shooters. A helicopter. Next thing we'll have fucking armored cars coming out of our asses."

Ilse had never heard her like this before. "Are you OK, ma'am?"

Anja glared at her as though she didn't have any right to ask the question. "Just concentrate on your job. Get Jake out of there, now."

Ilse turned back to the screen. "Jake, you've got a helicopter coming in from the north."

———

"I LOVE it when you talk dirty to me," Hawk growled as he jogged across the train line towards a cluster of houses. "How far out?"

"Maybe, two mikes."

"Now I'm really excited."

He kept running across the open ground before slotting into a narrow alleyway between two buildings. He paused for a moment and looked back. Three shooters appeared as they followed his footsteps towards the train line. Hawk brought the G36 up to his shoulder and sighted through the dot sight. It centered on the first man's chest, and he squeezed the trigger.

The man dropped into the dirt and the two beside him followed him to the ground. Realizing that they were in the open, there was nothing they could do except take cover.

Just that one shot was enough to buy Hawk more time, and he whirled and ran into the maze that was between all the houses. As he traveled, he could hear the whop, whop of the helicopter blades as it drew closer.

Hawk pressed himself up against the wall of a building as the helo flew overhead. He could see one of the crew manning a minigun in the right-side door as it passed over.

"Can you hear me, Jake?"

"Got you."

"Head east, the buildings get a lot denser in that region."

"Copy."

———

"MA'AM, I have an ID from one of the images we captured," Karl said.

"Show me," Anja replied.

The picture came up and Karl gave her the basics. "Rolf Balzer. Former Black Ops, led his own team for three years—"

"Before he was killed in a failed operation in the Congo, two years ago," Anja finished for him. "I know him. Worked with him before. The mission he was killed on was the second I ever commanded. Before I took command of the special operations branch, I was a field operative. That was where I first met him. He looks pretty good for a dead man."

"I had discovered that, yes."

"They must have a communication system. Find it."

"Yes, ma'am."

"Ilse, how is Mister Hawk faring?"

"He seems to be moving further away from them," Ilse replied.

"Keep an eye on him. Vector Mister Harvey to a new location to intercept."

"Yes, ma'am."

"I found the signal," Karl said to Anja.

"Put it on the speaker."

At first there was static, but it was followed by voices speaking German. They all listened intently. They had no idea where Hawk had disappeared to and were widening the search.

Anja asked Karl, "Can you break into their traffic?"

"I think so."

"Then patch me in."

A few moments later, Karl said, "Go, ma'am."

"Hello, Rolf. It's been a while."

"Who is this?" the man sounded irritated.

"Oh, come on, don't you know the voice? Unless of course being dead has also made you deaf."

"Anja?" He sounded confused.

"It's me."

"What—how?"

"My people are good," she explained. "In fact, you're chasing one of them now. Be careful, he bites."

"I can see that. I might have figured he was one of yours."

"I have a proposition for you, Rolf," Anja said.

"I'm listening."

"Call your people off and we meet face to face. Talk for a while, figure things out. What do you say?"

"Why would I do that?" Balzer asked.

"Because you're curious. You always were. Besides, I have a UAV overhead and with one word I could make your death permanent."

"You're bluffing, Anja. You forget that I know you. If you had an asset overhead, you would have used it by now."

"Are you willing to take the risk that I'm not?" Her voice was calm, unreadable.

There was a long silence before Balzer said, "All right. I'll meet with you."

"When and where?"

"There is a market on the west side of Dodoma. It is in a square. There is a small coffee shop. I'll meet you there in the morning."

"I'll look forward to it."

"There is one other thing. You have a friend of ours."

Anja said, "If you look in the back of the Land Rover, I think you will find him. Just know it wasn't my man."

A moment of silence and Anja could tell that the former black ops commander was stewing. Then he said, "I will see you tomorrow, Anja."

The Talon commander made a slashing motion across her throat and Karl killed the link. She looked at Ilse. "Let's see what he does."

As they watched, the shooters looking for Hawk started to fall back. "Looks like it's working, ma'am," the intel officer said.

"Good."

"You want to tell me what that was all about?"

Anja stared at her. "No. Just get Jake back here."

CHAPTER TWO

Democratic Republic of the Congo, Two Years Earlier

SWEAT COURSED down between Anja's breasts as she reached her climax atop Rolf Balzer. The German team commander reached his own just as she did, their cries filling the room, bouncing off the terracotta-colored walls of the hotel in the capital city, Kinshasa.

Minutes later after they had returned from the dizzying heights of ecstasy, Anja rolled off Balzer and lay beside him, her head resting on the pillow. "We need to stop this," she said to him, her body still covered in a thin sheen of perspiration from the humidity of the room.

"How?" he asked her. "You are addictive like cocaine."

Anja chuckled. "You exaggerate, Rolf."

He rolled onto his side and traced a finger around one of her erect nipples. A handsome man, Rolf carried an element of arrogance which is what had attracted her. His hair was blond, his jaw square, his eyes blue. "Do I? Tell me you don't feel it, too."

She couldn't because she did. She felt every bit of it, and it was becoming distracting. "After this mission, Rolf, there will be no more. You will replace Franz's team in

South America. There is something happening on the Triple Frontier. I need a good team down there."

His hand stopped moving. "So that's it? Just like that?"

"It has to be. Now that I'm commanding the Special Operations Branch I can't afford to be distracted."

"But it was all right before," he snapped and moved away from her.

"I'm sorry."

Anja felt his tension through the mattress as Balzer stiffened. She knew he was about to take it further when the cell beside the bed buzzed. She rolled to grab it and as she did, heard Balzer's cell go, too. She picked it up and answered, "Meyer."

"We're on."

"I'll be right there."

She disconnected and looked across at Balzer. "We're good to go."

"It would seem so."

Anja stared at him. "Are you alright, Rolf?"

"I'm fine," he grunted.

"Is this going to affect your performance on the job?"

"Has it done so yet?"

She left it there.

———

"THE TEAM IS WHEELS UP, Miss Meyer, and should be over the drop zone in fifteen minutes," the intel officer said from his work console.

"Thank you, Dedric. Eva, is the target still onsite?"

"Yes, Miss Meyer."

"Fine. Keep an eye on the situation and update Rolf once his team is on the ground."

The target Anja was talking about was a Dutch arms dealer, Gust Jansen. He was in the DRC arming rebels for another civil war which was bubbling away below the surface. It was something that the UN couldn't allow to happen, not with everything going on in the world, so they turned to Germany for help after the British and Americans, even the French, were tied up with their own hotbeds of violence. The mission was passed along to Anja and her group who brought in Rolf Balzer and his team of specialists.

Within days they were all in country prepping for the mission. Now it was operational.

Anja straightened. "Listen up, people. We're not far out from kicking off with boots on the ground. I want total concentration on the situation at hand. Anything looks out of place, I want to know. It doesn't matter how small. We know there is a battalion-sized force of rebels in the area and the last thing our people on the ground want is to stir up a hornets' nest. This will be a precision operation. That is all."

———

THE SMALL VILLAGE looked almost deserted from the ISR feed, and Anja felt uneasy. "Keep an eye out for anything that looks out of place," she told her people.

"Blue Team in position," Balzer's voice came over the comms.

Anja looked at the feed. "We have you on ISR. Looking good."

"Setting up an OP. We'll wait for dark and then go in," the team commander replied.

"Copy."

"Miss Meyer, I have movement approximately five-hundred meters south of Blue Team's position."

Anja's heart jumped. "Show me."

The screen changed and a picture of the jungle came up in its place.

"Come on, Dedric, you can do better than that."

"Sorry."

The screen changed once more and five pale figures could now be seen. Anja stared at it. They were spread out, moving slowly. Like military. "I want a wide shot of that now," she snapped.

Again, the screen changed, and she heard one of her people gasp. The number of figures had just changed from five to around five-hundred. "Get Blue Team out of there. Abort mission. Scramble the helos. I want the lift helicopter and the gunship in the air now."

Radio transmissions started to go out immediately as she heard her people calmly doing their jobs.

"I want to hear what's going on. Put it on speaker."

The four speakers placed around the ops room came to life and Anja started to filter through the intel coming in.

"Blue One is moving..."

"Blue Two going left..."

"Blue Four, on me..."

"Blue One, the X-Rays are closing your position..."

Anja's eyes narrowed. "What is Blue One doing?"

"I don't know, Miss Meyer."

"Blue One, sitrep, over."

Static.

"Blue One, this is Alpha One, sitrep, over."

"Say again, Alpha One. I'm getting a lot of interference, over."

Damn it, Rolf. "Blue One, sitrep, over."

Nothing.

"Blue Two, copy?"

"Yes, ma'am," came the reply.

"What is Blue One doing?"

"He ordered us to leave while he set up a welcome for them, ma'am."

"What do you mean a 'welcome,' Blue Two?"

"He's placing some claymores."

19

"Damn it."

Suddenly the screens went blank. "What just happened? Somebody, talk to me now!"

No one answered for a moment.

"I need someone to tell me what just happened."

"We've lost ISR feed, ma'am," came a voice.

"Well, get it back up."

"We are trying but it could be interference by an outside source."

Through the static which replaced the radio traffic came the distorted sound of voices and shooting.

"Can we get through to them?" Anja asked.

"No, Miss Meyer."

"Then why the hell can we hear them?"

"I don't know."

"Shit. Find me a quick reaction force. Reach out to the Congolese Army. I think they've got a battalion ten kilometers south."

For the next few minutes, they tried to regain contact with their field team but their efforts were fruitless. "Someone, tell me something."

"I can't raise the exfil helicopter."

"What about the army?"

"They're not moving. They say intelligence has three thousand rebel troops in the area."

Anja whirled on the speaker. "That's bullshit. Who told them that?"

"No idea, ma'am."

"Well, straighten them out."

"I tried. They're adamant and not moving."

"Shit. Put me through."

"They're not picking up. I already tried."

Everyone stared at Anja, expecting her to give them an order to make everything all right. But how could she? Their communications were down, the Congolese army refused to help, what was there that was left? "Get me General Fontaine."

Claude Fontaine was the commanding officer of the UN peacekeeping force in the country. He was aware of the presence of Anja and her team for he was the one who'd passed the intelligence along looking for a country willing to take the mission.

"The general is on the line, Miss Meyer."

She picked up the phone on the desk beside her and hit a button. "General?"

"Anja, what can I do for you?"

"I need your help. I've just had a team ambushed in the field. My radio communications are down, and the Congolese army is refusing to help because they think there are more rebels in the area than there actually are."

"I guess you do. Give me a couple of minutes. Have someone send me your team's coordinates."

"On their way, sir." Anja disconnected. "Someone send the team coordinates to UN HQ."

Five minutes later, Fontaine called back. "You're in luck. There is a US Recon team in country close by that we have on loan. I've had them diverted. Their commander will reach out when he's close to the target area. His callsign is Cobra One."

"You forget that my comms are down, Claude. Someone has taken them out."

"A radio set will arrive there soon. We'll go old school. Good luck."

Anja looked at her watch. Thirty minutes since the op had blown up. They'd be lucky if any of them were still alive.

———

Gunnery Sergeant John "Reaper" Kane stabbed at the point of the small map with a grimy finger. "That's where they are. About two klicks from where we are."

"So we're going into the lion's den," a thickset, dark-haired man beside him said. "Hell of a way to finish your last mission out here in the Dark Heart, Reaper."

"Would you have it any other way, Tank?" Kane asked.

"Fuck no. I'm sick of playing ass end Charlie. We've been at it for the best part of five days. Time to have some fun."

Five days. Tank Holman was right. They'd been creeping through the jungle for most of that time marking trails and rebel camps without even so much as a shot being fired. All that was about to change.

"We'll put Hooker on point and Hammer will take rear security. Let's move."

For the next hour and a half, in spite of the urgency, they made their way with a certain caution into the operational area of the German team. Everything was quiet. Spent casings were scattered around the jungle floor and some of the foliage had been cut down by bullet strikes.

"Everyone spread out," Kane said in a low voice.

The four men searched the area for a few minutes before they came back together. "What do we have?" Kane asked.

"A shitload of empty cases," Hammer said.

"It looks like they lit out to the east," Hooker told them. "Three of them."

"There was meant to be four."

"The village looks empty," Tank said.

Kane nodded. "Let's have a look. Hooker, Hammer, follow the trail east for a piece. Not too far though. I don't want the rebels coming back and dividing us."

"Roger that."

"I guess I'd better reach out to our German friends. Alpha, this is Cobra One, over."

"Read you loud and clear, Cobra One."

"Roger, Alpha. We're at the target area. No sign of your MIAs. Will check the village before moving on, out."

"Roger. Out."

Kane and Tank moved cautiously into the village. Both men were armed with M6A1s. As Tank had told him, the village was empty. They reached a small, cleared area in the center of it. It was there they found the remains of a wooden frame. It was still smoldering and tied to it was the blackened corpse.

"Somebody had a barbeque," said Tank. "Whoever it was, looks like he's well done."

Kane nodded. "Just keep an eye on my back while I have a look."

The sight was ghastly; roasted flesh fallen away from what had once been a man. Now it was unrecognizable. The sun glinted off something off to his right. Kane walked over to it, looked down at his feet, bent, and then retrieved it. It was a set of dog tags. He held them up in front of his face, the slight breeze making them move in a circular motion. Reaching out with his other hand, he stopped it and then read the name on them. Rolf Balzer.

"I think this is one of theirs," he said to Tank.

Kane stuffed the dog tags into his pocket. "Come on, let's catch up to the others."

They left the village and headed east into the jungle. Twenty minutes later, they caught up with Hammer and Hooker. "You find something back there?" asked Hooker.

"What was left of something," Kane replied. "What do you have?"

"Same three guys heading east."

"Are they being followed?"

23

"Not that I can tell. I mean, if there was a heap of rebels after them, you'd see it."

Kane looked into the jungle to their left and then to their right. "Hooker, left flank. Tank, right. I find it hard to believe that they haven't gone after them. Sweep the area. There's something out there. You need to find it."

Five minutes later, it was Tank that found what Kane had alluded to. "Cobra one, copy?"

"Roger, send traffic."

"You need to see this."

"On my way."

Kane found Tank amongst some thick jungle. Before the big Recon Marine said anything. Kane could see why he wanted him there. "They are moving parallel to the trail. I'd say maybe a hundred."

"All right, we need to move it up. They'll be trying to get ahead of them so they can spring another ambush."

For the next couple of hours, they followed the trail of the three remaining men from the German team. It wasn't until Hammer waited for him that Kane knew they were close. "Any minute now, Reaper," he said in a low voice.

Kane didn't question his man because he knew he was right. Hammer always had a sixth sense when something was about to happen. Then word came from Hooker on point. "Reaper, I've made contact."

He looked at Hammer and said, "Part bloodhound, aren't you?"

"Mama thought so."

The remaining German operators were in reasonably good health. One carried an upper arm wound but other than that all was well.

"What happened?" Kane asked Schultz, the man in charge.

"Shit happened. We lost our comms, our satellite link, and got hit by a numerically superior force. The only thing we could do was bug out."

Kane reached into his pocket and took out the tags belonging to Balzer. He handed them over and Schultz looked at him. "Dead?"

The big American nodded. "Yeah."

"Reaper, we need to move," Tank said. "The rebels are closing in on our position. A helo is picking us up at an LZ two klicks south of here."

Kane looked at the German. "Are you ready to go?"

"What about Balzer?"

"He's dead, he won't care."

———

Dodoma, Tanzania, Present Day

But he wasn't dead. He was here in Tanzania and just as alive as he had been back then.

"Are you sure this is a wise idea?" Hawk asked Anja. "If it was up to me—"

"It's a good thing it's not then, isn't it?" The tone of her voice was terse.

"Are you still pissed at me about the target?"

"What do you think?"

He stared at her. He usually liked to pick his battles but this one wasn't going away any time soon. Deal with it now. "It wasn't my fault."

"Of course you'd say that." There was bitterness in her voice this time.

"I forgot, I'm meant to be a mind reader."

"All you had to do was keep him alive, Jake."

"Yes. I should have seen them coming. Especially the friend of yours who is meant to be *fucking dead!*"

"Don't be a bloody child, Jake," Anja growled.

"I'm being a child? That's rich."

"Elaborate."

"Things didn't go right on the op. Shit like that

fucking happens. It's nobody's fault. Some things you can't foresee. I did my best. I didn't kill him. Put your dummy back in the cot and move on. Like I said, it is nobody's fucking fault."

Anja stared at him for several moments. "You're right. I'm sorry."

"Do we kiss and make up?"

"Don't push it."

"What do we do about your friend?" Hawk asked.

"You do nothing," she replied. "I've got Karl trying to ID some people and Ilse is attempting to find out where they are hiding."

"That can't be easy."

"No. You can help her if you wish."

He winced. "Me and computers—"

"Are fine. You're quite competent, even if you would rather get shot at."

"Easier to understand a bullet. You get shot, you die. Not much can go wrong there. There's a lot can go wrong with a computer."

"Get out of here."

"Yes, ma'am."

CHAPTER THREE

Dodoma, Tanzania

"WHAT HAVE WE GOT, HELGA?" Hawk asked Ilse as he sat at the console next to her.

"Good one, Sir Tugsalot."

"What?" he asked with a wry smile.

"Helga was from Sweden. I'm German, remember?"

"Minor geographical technicality."

"What do you want, Jake?" Ilse asked. "You've come to the wrong place if you expect me to rescue you from Anja."

"That ship has sailed. No, I came to see if I could help."

"Really?"

"Yes, really. Don't look so suspicious."

"It's the only thing I can be."

"Oh, ye of little faith."

Ilse touched the screen and swiped right. Instantly the one in front of Hawk lit up. He stared at it and said, "I'll never get used to that shit."

"We're looking for any sign of where these people might be holed up. So far, we've got not much."

27

"What about this scouser the boss knows?" Hawk asked.

Ilse nodded. "I've been running facial rec on the limited number of cameras throughout the city but I've come up with zero. It would help to know what name he was using."

"Next time I see him I'll ask," Hawk said with a grin.

"Idiot."

Hawk sighed. "Yes, but I'm your idiot."

"Good grief."

Thirty minutes later, Karl appeared. He looked troubled as he placed six folders on the desk near Ilse. "This is trouble."

Hawk stopped and glanced over. Ilse stared at Karl who was sanitizing his hands, his OCD seemingly heightened. It happened when he got nervous. "What is?"

"I've managed to identify six men from the ISR feed."

"And?"

Karl picked up the first folder and opened it. "Jonas Adler. Killed Afghanistan, Twenty-Eleven."

He dropped it and picked up the next. "Orlan Kessel. Killed North Africa, Twenty-Sixteen. Horst Banes, drowned in a training accident off the French coast. Body never recovered. Elbert Fenzel, died in a plane crash, Twenty-Eighteen. Even the other two. Every single one of them is dead."

Hawk nodded. "Never good when dead people are walking around."

Ilse said, "Find out if they had any family. Maybe they were chosen to die for that reason."

"Do we know if Balls had family?" Hawk asked.

Ilse gave him a funny look. "Balls?"

"Balzer. Balls. See?"

She shook her head. "Only you, Jake."

"He never," Karl replied to the question.

"So, Hermann the German—"

"Jake," Isle said, glaring at him.

"So, Hermann the German politician goes around recruiting dead operators and makes them his own private army. The question is for how long and how many?" He looked at Karl. "Did our canary tell the boss how long Hermann has been in the trafficking game?"

"Six years, supposedly."

"All right, have a look and see how many military personnel have died, or disappeared presumed dead, or body not recovered."

"What are you thinking, Jake?" Ilse asked.

"I'm trying to get a rough figure of dead people he could have working for him."

"I'll get back to you when I have something," Karl replied.

"One other thing, Karl," Hawk called after him. "See if you can dig up any known contacts in the local government that Hermann has frequent dealings with. He has to have in-country help from somewhere."

"You could be right. I'll start sifting through it."

"Call me when you've found something," Hawk said.

"Call?" Ilse questioned. "Are you going somewhere?"

"That's right."

"Where, might I ask?"

"To have a beer."

"Jake, I don't think that this is quite the time to go off drinking."

He said, "I'm going looking for our friends from today."

"You think they will be in a bar?"

"Most likely not, but there are always one or two that consider themselves an exception to the rule."

"But where do you start looking?" Ilse asked.

He looked at her and grinned. "Soldier, remember?"

———

ILSE SHOOK her head as the topless waitress walked past, her pendulous black breasts swaying with each step she took. Hawk placed his beer upon the scarred tabletop and said, "You didn't have to come."

"And leave you alone in a place like this?"

A different waitress came up to them, this one was a lot slimmer, her breasts smaller and sitting higher on her chest. "Would you like another drink?"

Ilse shook her head and Hawk said, "No, not at the moment."

"What about something else?"

The Talon intel officer suddenly realized that the waitress was talking to her. She could feel Hawk grinning at the situation and made a mental note to punch him in the mouth at the first opportune time. "No, thank you."

The woman pouted. "Pity. It's been a while since I entertained a white girl."

"She's just coming out of a messy relationship," Hawk told the waitress. "Her girlfriend was cheating."

Ilse glared at him.

"So sad, sweetie," the waitress commented before turning to Hawk. "How about you, handsome? You feel like hiding that sausage of yours?"

"Good grief, no," he blurted out. "You're way too much woman for me."

"You should let me prove it."

"Not tonight, love."

The waitress left and Ilse said, "My girlfriend was cheating?"

"Not a good excuse?" Hawk asked.

"Asshole," she growled. "You see anything?"

"Not yet."

Hawk kept scanning the bar. It was mostly filled with black people but there was the occasional white.

"Maybe we chose the wrong bar?" Ilse said.

"It's possible, but—" He stopped. Two men had just

entered. As he watched, the young woman who had just been at their table walked across the dimly-lit barroom with purpose. She greeted them and Hawk noticed that one of the men ran his hand up under her short skirt, cupping her buttock. "Those are the ones we want."

"How can you tell?"

Hawk ran a hand casually across his unshaven face and said, "They're military. I can smell it from here."

"Just because they were once military doesn't mean they're the ones we're after."

"Then I'd best find out," he said, getting to his feet.

"Jake, what are you going to do?"

"Like I said, find out."

Picking up his beer, he grinned at Ilse then turned and walked up behind the waitress standing beside a table where the two men had made themselves comfortable. He ran his hand up the back of her thigh and cupped her buttock. He then leaned forward and said, "Are you busy?"

"Hey, who the fuck you think you are?" one of the men asked with an unmistakable German accent.

Hawk held up his hands. "Hey, mate, I'm just trying to get a drink. And maybe something a little extra."

"Fuck off, she was with us first," the man snarled.

Hawk stared at him. The dark-haired man's brown eyes glittered angrily beneath his heavy brows. His sleeve had slipped up a little and Hawk could see the hint of a tattoo. The waitress turned and smiled at Hawk, her hand drifting across his groin, pausing for a squeeze before moving on. "I'll get your drink shortly, sweetie. Just go and have a seat."

"Fine," Hawk grunted, turning and walking away.

He sat back down at the table with Ilse who asked, "You have a good feel?"

"She's got tight buttocks, I'll give her that."

The intel officer rolled her eyes. "Well, what did you find out?"

"Both of them are German."

"And?"

"The waitress knows them rather well."

"So what is your next move?" Ilse asked.

"We're going to get a room."

"We are?"

Hawk grinned. "Yes, all three of us."

"Shit."

"Shh, here she comes."

"Now, sweetie, what was it you wanted?" the waitress asked.

"We've changed our minds, love," Hawk said. "Both of us."

She nodded knowingly. "Did you have anyone in mind?"

"You up for it?"

The waitress looked over her shoulder at the Germans and then at Ilse. She nodded. "All right, follow me."

They got up from the table and followed the waitress out the back, through a beaded curtain. From there it was up some stairs on the right to a second floor with pink painted walls, the only light covered with a red shade.

On either side of the hallway were doors, spaced symmetrically along the hallway, most of which were closed; of those, moans and cries of ecstasy could be heard emanating from within.

The waitress stopped at the end of the hallway and stood aside. She indicated the open door and said, "In here."

In the room was a large bed sitting on the carpeted floor, and a single cupboard. The waitress closed the door behind them and got down to business. "It will cost you one hundred dollars, American. I don't do anal, and I don't swallow. You get excited and shoot in my mouth and

I'll cut your balls off. If you're into that kind of thing, then do it to your girlfriend."

"So I guess you're open to chewing the one-eyed trouser snake then," Hawk said to her.

Ilse rolled her eyes once more.

"Shower first."

"I won't be needing that," Hawk said.

"No shower, no fun."

Hawk shook his head. "Yeah, nope, won't be needing the fun either."

The waitress gave him a funny look.

Hawk reached into his pocket and took out two hundred-dollar bills. "Here, this is for your time."

"What is this?" the waitress demanded.

The former SAS operator held out one of the notes. "Take it."

She took it and stared at him.

"That's for your time. The other is for some information."

The waitress held out the note to give it back. "No, I don't want it."

"Keep it," Ilse replied. "Like he said, it's for your time."

Hawk stared at her. "Those men downstairs. The Germans. Who—"

"I don't know." Her response was so rapid it cut him off.

Reaching into his pocket, Hawk took out another hundred. "This is all I have."

"I—"

"Just a couple of answers and then we'll leave," Ilse said in a quiet voice.

"They will kill me."

"We believe these men are part of a trafficking ring that are taking girls from Tanzania and sending them to

33

Belgrade in Serbia. We just need to know where they are staying."

A pained expression came across the waitress's face. "Why? Why me? Why not one of the other girls?"

"Because they fancy you," Hawk said. "And men like that talk."

Her shoulders slumped. "What if I do not wish to tell you?"

"Then we will leave," Ilse replied. "But a lot of young girls will die because of that one decision."

The girl's anguish caused tears to form in her eyes. "There—there is a place west of town. Many years ago, it used to be an old safari lodge. They are there."

Ilse nodded to her, a look of appreciation on her face. "Thank you."

———

"NO," Anja snapped. "I want to meet with Rolf first before we do anything."

"We have surprise on our side," Hawk persisted. "They won't even know we're coming."

"*We* don't even know how many there are," Anja pointed out.

"He's right, ma'am," Ilse said.

"But I'm in charge," she shot back, reminding them that this was her team.

"So we do nothing?" Hawk asked forcefully.

"Watch your tone, Mister Hawk. No, if you must do something, set up surveillance."

"Fine, I'll take Grizz—"

"Mister Harvey is on his way back to Hereford." The tone of Anja's voice was curt.

Hawk's eyes narrowed. "He's what?"

"The team is to front an enquiry about the death of Mac."

34

Ilse couldn't believe what she was hearing. "How can this be? They know we're on an operation."

"It is what it is. We make the best with what we have. Marcus is still here."

"Who's going to watch your back when you meet with Balzer?"

"I'll be fine."

"That's bollocks if I ever heard it," Hawk growled.

"You will follow orders, Jake." This time she was more forceful.

His jaw set firm. "Yes, ma'am."

Anja left them and Ilse looked at the former SAS operator. "We're not going to leave her out there on her own, are we?"

"Not on your life."

———

MARCUS GRAY WAS a former Para from the Regiment. He was Mac MacBride's replacement and had five years' experience in various combat zones. He was late twenties but looked to be nineteen. His dark hair was cut short, and he was fastidious in his presentation.

When Hawk and Ilse found him, he was in the middle of reassembling his CZ Bren2. Looking up from his work when they entered the room, Gray said, "This don't look like it's going to be a barrel of monkeys."

"Got a job for you if you're in," Hawk said. "It's below the radar and against orders."

"You'd better tell me what it is." The resigned look on his face spoke volumes.

Ilse explained what they wanted done and the former Para nodded. "I'm in."

"You'll have a comms link back to Karl. I'll see to that myself. But apart from that, you're on your own."

"What if something happens?"

"You're on the ground, you make the call. But no hero bullshit."

"Copy that."

———

IT WAS ALMOST noon when the meeting took place. Hawk and Ilse were already in position watching the old safari lodge. Meanwhile, Gray was sitting in a battered Mitsubishi van with his Glock 19 on his lap observing the outdoor seating at the cafe chosen for Anja to meet Balzer.

"Karl, do you have eyes on this?" Gray asked.

"Roger. What seems to be the trouble?"

"This whole setup. I can count at least four X-Rays and there are still no targets in play yet."

"That doesn't sound good. It could just be security."

"It could," Gray allowed as he looked at a man standing on the corner opposite with a newspaper. "But these pricks stand out like dogs' bollocks. I mean they should be in some city in Europe, not here. It's like they want to stand out."

"Wait one, I'll patch Jake and Ilse through."

A few moments later, Ilse came on. "What is it, Marcus?"

He explained what he was seeing.

"I agree," Ilse said. "We need to warn Anja."

Gray stared out the dirt-streaked window of the van. "Too late, she's here."

———

ANJA HAD PICKED them all out before she'd even reached the seating area of the café. Four of them and possibly one in the van. So, make it five.

She sat down at a table and a waiter came out to greet her. His smile revealed white teeth which stood out

36

against the background of his dark skin. "What can I get you?" he asked in halting English.

"Coffee, please."

With a courteous bow, he hurried away.

No sooner had he disappeared when another figure came out through the doorway. This time it was Balzer. "Hello, Anja."

She stared at him, her heart beating a little faster than before. "Hello, Rolf."

As he sat down, she noticed the handgun. "You won't need that. I'm sure you have enough men scattered around."

He smiled. "Still the same Anja."

"Not the same Rolf," she shot back at him.

"Things change," he replied.

"But what?"

"Money."

She nodded. "It's always money. And slavery pays well?"

"As well as one can hope."

"How did Hermann recruit you?" Anja asked.

"What?"

"Hermann. Wolfgang Hermann."

"I have nothing to do with him."

Anja thought for a moment before it dawned. Intel had Wagner as part of Hermann's organization. Leonid had said—he was playing her. "How silly of me. It wasn't Hermann, it was Medusa. This part is theirs. He's just a customer like the rest."

Balzer remained silent as the waiter returned and placed a coffee in front of Anja.

Once he was gone, she asked, "What did Wagner do?"

"You don't know?"

"Obviously our intel was wrong. We had him as a part of Hermann's ring. He's dead now, what does it matter?"

Balzer shrugged. "He was just a bookkeeper. An accountant."

"For what?" Anja asked. "Money? Numbers?"

"Shipping. He kept records of what went where and how much it cost. Last year alone there were one thousand units of merchandise passed through here."

Anja paled. "One thousand girls?"

"Girls and men."

"They all went to Hermann?"

Balzer shrugged. "To him, his different business interests."

The figure was frightening. But what was even more frightening was the fact that Medusa was capable of supplying that number.

"I don't suppose you know where Ilya Noskov is? He disappeared after he killed Viktor Medvedev."

"No idea."

She looked into his eyes. "You're lying, Rolf. I could always tell. That's how you knew we were here."

"They do have good intelligence services," Balzer replied. "There's not much that they don't know."

Anja's eyes flared with anger. "Damn it, Rolf, why?"

"We already know the answer to that."

"When then? When did they approach you?"

"Not long before the last deployment to the Congo. They organized everything. I just had to be there."

"You bastard, do you know what you did? How it made me feel. I lost you. I lost the man I loved."

"I'm sorry."

"Fuck you," she hissed.

He stared at her. "What are you doing here, Anja?"

"You already know that, Rolf."

"I can't let you interfere. You've already killed an important link."

"That was your people."

"Even so..."

"How are you going to stop it? Kill me?"

"If I have to." His eyes were cold, soulless. "Just take your people and leave, Anja. It's easy. Just forget about it."

"Forget about all the girls that you kidnap and sell into sexual slavery?" Her voice was incredulous.

"I don't sell them. I just do my job."

"It's a shit job."

"Which pays a lot better than what the German government ever did."

"I can't believe you've..." She was at a loss for words.

"I'll give you twenty-four hours to get out of Tanzania, Anja. After that I'll forget we were lovers and do what I have to do."

"Which is?" Anja asked.

"Kill every last one of you."

"Is that what Noskov wants?" Anja snarled. "Well, you tell him this. We're not leaving. And we won't stop until the whole stinking castle that Medusa has built is brought crashing down. Brick by fucking brick."

Balzer chuckled. "No. Ilya doesn't care about you. This is like a game to him. You tear down a piece here, he will rebuild over there. He is much different to Viktor."

"I'm sorry it has come to this."

"Me, too," Balzer said and stood up. It was a prearranged signal for it was at that moment his men moved.

CHAPTER FOUR

"SOMETHING IS WRONG," Gray said in a calm voice, grabbing the Glock.

"Tell me what you see," Karl said.

"She stood up to leave but they're closing in on her. I think they mean to take her."

"All right, keep an eye on them. I'll let Ilse and Jake know."

"Fuck that," Gray growled. "I'm going to do something."

"Gray, don't."

"Been nice knowing you, Karl."

The former Para climbed out of the van and glanced around. There were four outriders. He'd been right about that. Now they were closing on Anja and Balzer.

As he started slowly along the street towards the café, he had the advantage of coming up behind two of them. Now, any gentleman would give his enemy a sporting chance. *Fuck that. Put them down fast and put them down hard.*

The Glock came up and Gray opened fire. Twice at the first man, twice at the second. Both went down and never moved. Somewhere amongst the crash of gunshots he heard Anja cry out his name, but he ignored it.

By now, Balzer's men were responding. The remaining two outriders were starting to focus on the new threat. Gray fired at the third of the four, but he was moving fast and both shots missed.

The fourth man opened fire, sending Gray running for cover behind a parked vehicle. Bullets punched into it and glass shattered. He rose and fired at the fourth man, seeing him flinch as the rounds passed close.

"Gray, behind you!" The warning came through his comms.

The former Para turned and saw two more men appear. The bastard had others. He fired his Glock at them as he propelled left towards a storefront. Diving into the open front door he rolled onto his back.

A figure loomed large in the opening, framed by the sunlight from outside.

BLAM! BLAM! BLAM! Three shots buried themselves deep into the killer's chest and he rocked back on his heels before falling into the dirt outside.

"Gray, there's another approaching your position," Karl said urgently.

"Bollocks," Gray growled as he noticed that his weapon was empty. He dropped out the magazine and replaced it with a fresh one.

No sooner had he finished when the second shooter appeared. This time the figure in the doorway got off a shot just as Gray fired. The former Para hissed in pain as the bullet from the killer burned a deep furrow along his upper left arm.

Gray fired again and this time the shooter fell on top of his comrade. The former Para scrambled to his feet and edged to the doorframe. He peered around it and bullets peppered the front of the store.

Suddenly he became aware of the alarmed cries behind him. He turned but could see nothing but the battered wooden counter. He hurried across to it and peered beyond. Three people, a man and two women, were hunkered down behind it. On catching sight of the man staring down at them, their cries became more urgent. "Stay down," he warned them. "You'll be fine if you do."

He rushed back to the doorway and looked out once more. There was no more shooting coming his way. Keeping low, Gray moved along the shopfront towards the café. He was just in time to see the remaining men disappear inside with Anja.

Gray's pace quickened as he broke into a jog heading towards the open doorway. The former Para braced himself for a fusillade of gunfire, but nothing eventuated. He rushed into the cafe but saw that the eating area was devoid of any other souls.

Hearing the back door slam shut, he hurried past the serving counter and through a swinging door that led to the kitchen. This was empty as well. It was obvious that Balzer had the cafe evacuated before the meeting.

From the rear of the building, he heard the roar of an engine. Gray ran out the back door to see two vehicles driving away in a cloud of dust. He swore loudly and then said into his comms, "Karl, they've gone, and they've got the boss. I say again, they've got the boss."

———

ANJA GLARED AT BALZER, who sat beside her. "You know they won't stop until they get me back, don't you?"

The man nodded. "That's what I'm counting on."

"You're a bastard."

"I didn't want it this way, Anja," Balzer said. "All I wanted was for you to walk away, but you wouldn't do that. Now we have to do it this way."

"You seem to underestimate my people. As I said, they won't stop until they get me back. But in doing so, they will kill every man that you have."

He stared into her eyes, trying to read her thoughts. "You seem to have a lot of confidence in your people."

"Oh, I do. I just hope you have the confidence in yours. Because the past two days have just been a taste of what is coming your way. Think about that."

———

THE TEAM all gathered back at their HQ. Hawk and Ilse were on the way to the café so all they had to do was redirect.

"What do we know?" Hawk asked.

"I did my best, Jake, but it wasn't good enough," Gray said as Ilse bandaged his arm.

"You made it count, Marcus. All we have to do now is get her back."

"They'll be expecting us," Ilse pointed out.

"Maybe we can use it to our advantage," Hawk replied. "Karl, did they take her to the lodge?"

"Yes."

"Right, then that's where we hit them."

"You seem to forget. Grizz and his team, apart from Marcus, are in the air on their way back to England," Ilse reminded him.

"Marcus and I can handle it."

Ilse looked skeptical. "Jake—"

"I'll be fine, ma'am," Gray said. "I'm Para, remember? Us blokes live behind the lines, surrounded and without hope. It'll be nothing new."

"Damn it, Jake," Ilse pressed. "We need to wait for reinforcements. I'll call the general."

Hawk looked at the other two men. "Give us a moment, lads."

43

They left the room and he stared at Ilse. "I can understand your reservations, Ilse, I really can. But if we wait then we run the risk of losing her."

"But what about Marcus?"

"Don't worry about Marcus. He is the real deal. I talked to Grizz. This guy was awarded the Military Cross in Somalia when an escort he was commanding got cut off by some bastard warlord who was set on wiping them out. He saved them all virtually single-handed."

She stared thoughtfully at him for a long moment before nodding. "All right, Jake. You're in the field. Your call."

"I wouldn't be doing it if I didn't think it could be done. I am going to need some things though."

"I'll get you what I can."

The door opened and Karl appeared, a worried expression on his face. "We have another problem."

He held up a piece of paper and presented it to the intel officer. Ilse took it and started reading. "It's from Hank Jones. Grizz and his team are being permanently reassigned."

"Be fucked," Hawk growled.

She passed over the message. He read it and a fire started to burn in his eyes. "Get me Thurston on a fucking line. This bullshit has got to stop."

Three minutes later, a voice said, "Jake—"

"Are you behind it?" Hawk snapped.

"Let me talk to Anja," former general Mary Thurston said.

"I can't, you'll have to talk to me. Tell me why Grizz's team is getting reassigned."

"What do you mean, I can't? Put her on, Jake." This time the voice was firmer.

"I can't because she's been taken captive by an old friend of hers."

"Don't fuck me around, Jacob. You put her on the call now."

"I'm not fucking you around. She met with the guy earlier today and he decided he liked her more than what we did. We're in the middle of planning a rescue when this message comes through about Grizz. So, General, what the fuck?"

"For starters, Jake, it's only for the three of them, not Gray. He remains with you. And as for the reason why, Anja was told to trim the fat from her team so to speak. Or we would do it for her. She chose Harvey and his team because they couldn't really be split up. They will now work for Global in another capacity."

"Is that what they were going back to Hereford for?" Hawk asked.

"Yes."

"Bollocks."

"Tell me about this rescue attempt."

"We've got it covered," Hawk said and hung up.

Hawk's arm came back and was about to propel the phone across the room when Ilse's voice stopped him. "Jake!"

"What?"

"It's not the phone's fault."

"Yeah, well..."

"What did she say?"

"She said the boss was asked to trim the fat from the team," he explained. "She picked Harvey and the other two. Gray stays with us. I presume to help me in the field."

"So we're it?"

"Yeah."

"Then we better work out a plan to get Anja out of there."

THE FOUR OF them stood around an A3 sized satellite photo of the old safari lodge and its surrounding buildings. Karl poked the grainy black and white picture with a pen. "They have the boss here."

Hawk looked at the small building. "Out in the middle of nowhere. What does that tell you?"

"That it's the biggest dog's breakfast going," Gray said.

Karl continued. "They have guard posts here, here, here, and here. Two roving patrols which could double at night. They look like they use this building as a barracks." His pen kept jumping. "Shower block, mess, machine shop, plus the others. I'd be guessing what they were. They have cameras there, there, there, there, and there."

"Regular little outpost," Hawk said. "Where do they draw their power?"

"From the main line. But I'm guessing that they have generator backup."

"Hold it," Ilse said. "Let's assume they have girls onsite. Where do they keep them?"

They all went quiet.

Hawk said, "So, we're going in ninety-five percent blind."

"We have to know where they are if you want any kind of aircover," Ilse said.

"Just hit the targets we know," Hawk said.

"That's not how it works, Jake."

"I saw a Hornet in the kit," Gray said. "Why don't we use that to snoop around before we go in?"

The Hornet he was referring to was a Black Hornet Nano. It was a Micro Unmanned Aerial Vehicle.

"Can you fly it?" Hawk asked.

"Yes, sir."

The former SAS operator looked at Ilse. "If we can find the building they're in, *if* they're there, we can mark it before the UCAV unloads on the place."

The UCAV was an Unmanned Combat Aerial Vehicle. The one they were going to use was a General Atomics MQ-9 Reaper.

"Jake, if you can't get a PID on them, the airstrike diversion will be off. No ifs or buts."

"If we don't get the strike, we don't get the boss. Karl counted—how many X-Rays, Karl?"

"Thirty."

"Thirty X-Rays. Do you know how many that is?"

Ilse nodded. "I can count, Jake, and the order still stands."

Hawk didn't like it, but he understood. "Yes, ma'am."

"You'd better get ready. It won't be long before it'll be dark. You need to be in position."

Hawk turned away and started to walk.

"Be careful out there, Jake. These people are deadly."

"I guess they haven't met Mrs. Hawk's little boy," he countered.

———

"ARE you sure you can fly this bloody thing, Marcus?" Hawk asked picking up the miniature helicopter-like UAV.

"Just as long as my asshole points to the ground," he replied. "We used to use them every now and again in the Paras. Good little units, they are."

"Is it going to be able to do the job?"

"Fuck yeah. These things are like dynamite, mate. Haven't you ever used one before? Not in the SAS?"

"Not in my troop. We used to use the big fuckers, mate. Send a decent message."

"Well, you're about to learn something, Jake."

Gray set up the station and got the little machine ready. He checked it over once before handing it to Hawk. "Put it up for me, mate. We'll get this thing going."

Hawk held his arm up straight above his head, and

within moments the little UAV was humming as its motor wound up. "Let it go."

The former SAS operator released the little UAV and it darted upwards, disappearing into the darkness. Gray concentrated on the screen as he used the small one-handed remote to guide the machine towards the compound.

"Shit," Gray cursed. "Bloody gust of wind caught it. That's the only problem with these things. They're that light. You get a little bit of breeze and they can be tricky to handle."

"What's the flying time on this thing?" Hawk asked.

"Twenty minutes. We usually have him out for fifteen and that allows us five minutes to get him back home. All we have to do is press a button and they come back to us. But that's why there are two just in case we don't get it right on the first try."

Hawk looked down at the small screen. The Nano UAV seemed to be traveling across the ground quite well. "How high is it?"

"About twenty meters."

"And no one can hear it?"

"No. Even at that height, no one can hear anything. The best thing they did was add infrared and shit like that."

"You sound like you've got a hard on."

"You got it right there, mucker. I'm about to blow a hole in my pants."

"Save it for R&R. Just find us what we need." Hawk paused before saying, "Alpha Two, are you getting this feed, over?"

"Copy, Bravo One. Feed is coming through crystal clear."

"Roger that."

Hawk watched Gray weave his magic with the little machine. They could make out almost everything they needed to know but still they lacked the knowledge of where, if at all, any girls being shipped were being held.

"Try the bigger building to the west," Hawk said.

Gray maneuvered the Hornet into place. At first there was nothing and then the thermal imaging camera brought up the heat signatures of those within. "Looks like it could be it," Gray said.

"Is there any way you can get a better look?"

"Bear with me a second."

The Hornet buzzed lower until it was level with the building. Then through the camera, Hawk could see that it was approaching a window on the side. Just when it seemed it was about to crash into the glass, Gray brought it to a stop. He adjusted the focus, and they could see within the room itself, even though it was dark. The night vision capabilities came to the fore.

"That's them," Hawk said. "How many you figure there are?"

"Fifteen, maybe twenty."

"That's too many."

"What do you want to do?" Gray asked.

"We go after the boss. Use the UAV as a last resort."

"A wayward Hellfire would fuck up everybody's day?" After a moment of silence, he said into his comms, "Alpha Two, copy?"

"Read you, Bravo One."

"Place UAV on standby. We're going to try and get this done without having to use it. We have up to twenty friendlies in the building to the west. Wouldn't want to upset their night, over. We'll use the backup diversionary plan. We can pass the information on to the U.N. and they can send some people along to get them out."

"Copy, Jake. Will let the fly guys know of your intentions."

"Bravo One moving to insert, out."

By the time Hawk had signed off, Gray had the

Hornet back to the van. He packed it away and then they readied their equipment. Both men wore full tactical gear, including body armor, night vision, and extra ammunition for their suppressed Bren2s.

During their briefing and planning stage, they had found a tunnel from an old sewer system which went underneath the Safari Lodge compound. Looking at the plans, which were designed long ago, there were three outlets which they could use to come up above ground. One of which was within range of the building where they were holding Anja.

Hawk looked at Gray. "You ready, Mucker?"

"Let's get it done, old cock."

CHAPTER FIVE

Outside Dodoma, Tanzania

EVEN THOUGH THEY hadn't been used for years, the tunnels still smelled like stale shit. The two shooters slowly made their way through them, hunched over so not to hit their heads on the roof. Somewhere, a rat screeched in defiance at being disturbed by the pair.

"Thank fuck it is dry in here," growled Gray in a low voice. "I've been crawling through these things when they're fully loaded before and let me tell you, it's not pleasant."

Hawk said, "Try crawling through one in Italy with all the food that they eat. I swear I couldn't see for a week afterwards. My eyes were watering that much."

"Even worse when it splashes up into your mouth," Gray put forward.

"Yeah. OK, you win."

They kept moving until they reached their exfil position. Above them was a metal grate large enough for them to climb through. Hawk reached up and tried it. The grate came free, and he slid it aside.

His head appeared through the opening, and he

scanned the immediate area through the luminescent green haze of his NVGs. Everything looked clear. "Alpha Two, copy?"

"Copy, Bravo."

"We're at Dagger One, looking for a go, no go, over."

"Roger, Bravo. Mission is a go. Good luck. Will call them as I see them."

"Copy. Bravo passing Dagger One."

Both men came clear of the hole in the ground and paused before moving in the direction of the nearest building, crouched low. Once in its shadows they both stopped.

Gray edged up to the corner of the building and raised his NVGs to stop them flaring against the light of the floodlights. He peered around the corner and saw a man coming in their direction.

Gray edged back and let the Bren hang by its strap before drawing his combat knife. He steadied his breathing and waited in the shadows for the man to appear.

It all happened fast. The man appeared and Gray grabbed him from behind, the knife in his hand slicing deep across the throat while his other hand was clamped over the mouth.

Gray dragged him into the shadows where he bled out silently.

"Bravo, the generator backup is around one hundred meters east of your position."

"Copy. Moving to location," Hawk replied.

They moved silently through the shadows, and to the best of their abilities avoided anything that was lit. Eventually they reached the backup generator, a large diesel-driven machine. Within moments, they had the fuel line cut as well as the wires. Nobody would get it started any time soon.

"Moving to main target," Hawk said in a low voice.

Minutes later, they were in position. Hawk said, "Kill the lights."

Suddenly the whole camp went black as Karl cut the power.

"Move, Marcus," Hawk said.

Both men broke cover and started across the open ground towards the building where they knew Anja to be held captive. Ahead of him, Hawk heard Gray fire three rounds from his Bren.

Through the green haze, a man dropped to the ground, spilling his weapon from his grasp. "X-Ray down."

To Hawk's left another shooter appeared confused as he hurried through the darkness. The former SAS man stroked the trigger and his weapon spat death. "X-Ray down."

Shouts could be heard around the former Safari Lodge, as men were suddenly confused by the gunfire and the darkness. Still the two Talon operatives kept moving towards their target.

Over the comms Ilse's voice could be heard, "Looks like they're gathering around the Safari Lodge. Once they get organized, it won't take long for them to work out what's going on."

"Roger that."

The building loomed ahead of them. Outside stood two men. Hawk came out from behind Gray, and each picked their target. When they opened fire, they continued until both were down.

Hawk tried the door but found it locked. He kicked it hard, and it crashed back. "Are you in here, boss?"

"Jake, is that you?" the voice asked from within.

He broke a glow stick so she could see better. "Yeah, it's us. We've come to get you out."

"What are you doing here?"

"No time for pleasantries," he replied. Taking his

Glock from his thigh holster, he passed it to Anja. "Take this."

She took the weapon. "How did you find me?"

"We're good, remember?" A pause. "Alpha Two, we have the package. Proceeding to extract."

"Jake, just so you know, they're closing on your position, I think the jig is up."

"Copy. Understood."

Hawk turned to Gray. "Time for that distraction, old mate."

"Roger that." The former Para reached for a trigger in his pocket. A few moments later, a large explosion rocked the compound from the western side.

Hawk said, "Keep your hand on my ass, boss. We'll have you out of here in no time. Marcus, take point."

They exited the building and immediately turned east away from the explosion. Ahead of them, suddenly three men loomed up out of the darkness through the green haze. "Contact front!" Gray exclaimed, opening fire with his Bren.

The three would-be killers jerked violently with every impact of the bullets sprayed from the weapon. "X-Rays down, keep moving."

"Bravo One, you have a large gathering of hostiles coming in from your right."

Fuck it. "We need to speed it up. Marcus, cover right, I'll take point."

"On it."

Gray did a tactical reload as he moved, sweeping the area. The laser sight on the Bren2 reached out like a lance through the night. Then he saw them. Bunched up, coming their way. He flicked the selector to auto and opened fire. "Contact right."

Hawk turned and brought his own weapon into play. The bunched targets went to ground. Some dead, some dying, the rest responding.

Bullets cut through the darkness around the Talon team members. Hawk called over his shoulder, "Boss, get moving. We'll be right behind you."

Anja started moving once more towards the east, bullets fizzing and cracking all around. Behind her, she heard Hawk yell, "Peel back."

Then came, "Moving!"

Gray changed his position by fifteen meters before stopping. He then opened fire once more to cover Hawk as he peeled back.

"Changing!" Hawk shouted and reloaded beside the former Para. "Alpha Two, how are we looking on the extract?"

"Extract will be in position in two mikes. Move your asses."

"Come on, Marcus, time to move."

"On your six."

Suddenly above the gunfire came the sound of a revving engine. Headlights started to bounce in front of them as a vehicle came rocketing over the uneven ground towards them. "There's our ride," shouted Hawk.

The cargo van slid to a stop and the side door flew open, Karl filling the opening. "You like, want a ride?"

Anja was the first one in through the door. She skidded along to make room for the others. Gray stopped at the door, turned and opened fire at their pursuers, while Hawk leapt into the back of the van. "Come on, Marcus. Time to get out of here."

The former Para ducked into the back of the van and Karl slammed the door shut. Ilse floored the gas pedal and the van shot forward, its wheels spinning. Bullets peppered the thin side as they beat a hasty retreat. "Is everyone alright?" Ilse shouted back over her shoulder.

"All good here," Hawk shouted back. "How about you, boss? Are you OK?"

"I'm good. Keep driving."

As the van disappeared into the night, Rolf Balzer stood watching, his blood pressure starting to rise quickly. His plan had gone to shit, and Ilya Noskov wasn't going to be happy.

――――――

"WHAT THE HELL were you doing at the meet?" Anja growled at Gray. "You should have been nowhere near the place."

"He was trying to save your ass, boss," Hawk replied. "There is no reason why you should have been out there alone. And the fact that you got kidnapped proves that point."

"It was a foolish move. You could have got yourself killed."

"Well, he didn't."

Ilse said, "It was my call, I ordered him to do it."

"Well, you should have followed orders."

"If I had to make the choice, I'd do it all over again," Ilse said defiantly. "And speaking of foolish moves, that was one of them. There is no way you should have been out there on your own and I saw fit to make sure you weren't."

Anja glared at her for a moment and then nodded. "You're right. I guess I owe you all an explanation."

For the next five minutes, she gave them a brief outline of her relationship with Rolf Balzer. "I broke my number one rule. I got involved with a man I worked with. I should have seen it coming, but I didn't."

"Don't beat yourself up about it," Hawk said. "We're only human. Even if you try not to be."

"Thank you, Mr. Hawk. I think."

Karl appeared. "I called in the location of the safari compound and the fact that there were girls there to the UN. They've got men moving as we speak."

"I'm hopeful they'll find something," Gray said. "I hated leaving them behind."

Hawk slapped him on the back. "It was all we could do. Besides, tonight was a good mission. We got in, we got out. No casualties. The question is, what do we do now? Especially since we're down three of our own."

He stared at Anja, waiting for a response. She ignored it and said, "I learned that Rolf works for Medusa, not Hermann. Leonid conveniently left that important piece of intel out. I'll be talking to him about that to make sure he understands that game playing will not be tolerated. Meanwhile we need to work out the logistics of shipping their girls to Belgrade."

"The UN might dig up something," Hawk theorized.

"Maybe," Anja agreed. She looked to Ilse and Karl. "Get some rest first, then find me anything that even remotely looks like a thread we can use."

"Do you think it's time to cut the head off the snake?" Hawk asked.

"Yes, if we can get a fix on him, Jake, I promise you, I'll let you have a crack at him."

"I'll look forward to it."

———

"EVERYONE, gather around, the UN forces came through with intel," Anja said when she walked into the room. In her hands were some documents. "Papers to go through."

Every one of them gathered around. "What about the girls?" Gray asked.

"Incredibly, they were still there. They had been abandoned."

"Better than some," Hawk said, remembering others who had been killed so they couldn't divulge any information.

For the next hour, the team steadily pored through the documents, forming separate piles for different parts. It was Ilse that said, "There seems to be a few documents leading to a shipping company in Dar es Salaam."

Hawk said, "I've got some things here referring to the safari camp under a company name. Parkland Trading."

"I've got something about that here," Karl said. "Parkland Trading is a subsidiary of Rostov European Trading. What is the name of the shipping company?"

"Dittmar Lines."

"German name," Karl said and started tapping at keys on his computer. "Says here that Dittmar Lines has another office in Durres, Albania."

Hawk looked thoughtful. "They leave here, transit the Suez, then up to Durres. From there, Pristina then to Belgrade. Regular underground railway."

"Can we assume that the shipping company is somehow linked to Hermann?" Anja asked. "I mean being German one would think that it would be."

"I'll have to dig deeper," Karl replied, "but I would think it could be. As you are already aware, Medusa has fingers in many pies."

"I have a feeling that this is far from Medusa. Especially with the German connection."

Karl frowned as he stared at his computer. "There's something strange."

"What is it?"

"An account number for a Swiss bank. It looks like there was a substantial amount of money paid into it a short while ago."

All eyes turned to Karl. Hawk said, "Someone got careless. See who it belongs to."

Fingers danced and Karl let out a low whistle. "It's got five-hundred million dollars in it."

"What is the name of the account?" Anja asked.

"Rostov European Trading."

Silence spread across the room.

Anja said, "Empty it. Then hide it where no one can find it."

Ilse looked concerned. "Miss Meyer—"

"Think about it. The money has to belong to Medusa. The company is linked to the safari camp. That is linked to Medusa. If we seize the money, we keep it to fund our operations and in the process, maybe draw Noskov out of hiding. It is our chance of getting to him."

"What about the general?" Hawk asked.

"I'll fill her in. Do it, Karl."

A few taps and he said, "Done."

———

Somewhere in Europe

"No! No! No!" the young man gasped as he stared at his computer screen which flashed and screeched at him. "We have to stop it."

An older man with a balding head stood beside him, his face growing paler with every heartbeat. "We can't stop it."

Both men watched in silent horror as the last few electronic numbers ticked over and eventually settled on zero. "What do we do?" the young man asked.

"Shut that fucking alarm off so I can think."

The young man hit a button and the computer stopped screeching. Under a minute was all it had taken. From the time the account had been accessed to the time it had been emptied.

"Get out of the way," the older man snarled.

He sat down and started pounding the keys on the computer keyboard.

"What are you doing?"

"I'm trying to trace who it was that hacked the system."

"But they can't hack it. That was the way it was designed."

"Well, half a billion dollars just didn't get up and fucking walk out."

"This is bad."

Without looking up the older man said, "No, this is beyond bad. If we can't find it, we're both dead men."

————

ILYA NOSKOV STARED at the pair before him, his heart pumping liquid fire through his veins. "Five-hundred million dollars." His voice held a granite-like edge to it. "And you have no idea how it happened?"

"I—it just vanished," the younger man stammered. "We tried to trace it but—"

"The accounts are supposed to be secure. Is that correct?"

"Yes, sir."

"Then how did this happen?"

"There is only one way that it could have been possible," the older of the two men said. "Whoever did it had to have had the account number."

"And you could find no trace?"

"None."

"Two days."

The older man stared at him. "Pardon?"

"I give you two days to find the money. After that I will kill you, your families, your dog, cat, any fucking one who has had anything to do with you. I will kill them all."

"Yes—yes, sir."

They hurried out of the room, pulling the door closed quietly behind them.

A figure stepped out of the shadows of the darkened

room. Noskov turned and said, "It has to be them. I heard from Rolf Balzer earlier. It seems that he lost his prized possession. And now that part of the operation which supplied our client in Germany, too. These people are getting on my nerves. I want you to take a team to Belgrade and wait. They will follow the supply route to there. I know it because they are so resourceful. I will let our German friend know to expect them."

"Yes, sir," the figure replied.

Once more the door shut and Noskov leaned back in his chair. He closed his eyes and meditated, releasing the anger from his body.

———

Dar es Salaam, Tanzania

Hawk moved silently through the darkness between two stacks of shipping containers. He paused and listened for the security guard who was prowling the dock along with three others. Each one of them was armed.

The briny scent of the sea drifted on the air intermingled with the stink of fuel oil and garbage which had been dumped into the Mzinga Creek. Creek? River or inlet would have been a better description.

Hawk moved out into the open, glancing left and right. "Alpha Two, Bravo One, sitrep?"

"Looks clear, Jake."

Across the concrete pavement ahead of him, tied to the dock, was a large container ship, its appearance that of an oversized monster lurking in the water, its silhouette intimidating against the darkened sky.

In front of it was an office made from manufactured containers. This was Hawk's destination. What he was looking for was anything which would link the shipping line to Wolfgang Hermann.

He ran across the open ground and tried the door. It was locked but after twenty seconds of work, Hawk had the door open and was inside.

He turned on his flashlight and shone it around the large office. "Alpha Two, I'm in. Keep an eye out for any unwanted visitors."

"Copy."

Hawk moved about, trying for the obvious places first. Desks and drawers. He found a few papers but not really what he was looking for. Next, he moved to the filing cabinet, hoping that it would be unlocked. It wasn't, of course, and took him a few minutes to gain entry. Flicking through the files drawer by drawer, he eventually found something of interest. Two somethings, actually. A ledger, and a diary.

"Bravo, you have company headed your way," Ilse said over the comms.

Immediately Hawk killed the flashlight and moved to the window to look out. Two armed guards were walking towards the office. "Roger, Alpha Two. I have eyes on two X-Rays."

He watched their approach and as they drew level with the office, they stopped for a bit but continued the conversation they'd been having. Two minutes later, one of them suggested that they continue on their rounds and had taken several steps when the second guard spoke, stopping the progress of the first. He indicated towards the office and started moving towards the door.

Hawk grabbed his suppressed Glock and edged along to stand behind the door. He heard the handle turn and cursed himself for not locking it upon entry. The guard called to his friend and then opened the door.

Hawk made himself as small a presence against the wall—so the door would not hit him and bounce back, revealing that something was awry—the weapon in his hand ready to fire. As soon as the guard stepped through the opening, the former SAS man moved faster than a panther, shooting him point blank. Not satisfied with one, he kept walking until his frame filled the doorway and shot the second guard.

Then without stopping he crossed the open space towards the containers and slipped into the darkness.

———

Dar es Salaam, Tanzania

The ledger gave a rundown of money and shipments, the diary told them what those shipments were by the way of codes. For example, one shipment of stuffed toys cost $60,000 to ship, but their cost was double that. Going by the code in the diary, the stuffed toys were fifty women. Another shipment on a different ship cost $80,000 and once again the items, this time toy cars, were young men.

But the alarming figure was the one costing $200,000. This was for coffee. When Karl checked it against the code in the diary, he found out that they were families. "Twenty families," Karl said. "Men, women, and kids."

"What would they do with the kids?" Ilse asked.

"Adoption black market," Hawk said. "Big money from people desperate to have their own family."

"But surely the children would say something."

"Not if they were young enough."

"That's barbaric."

"It's all barbaric."

"Is there anything we can give Interpol to use as evidence against Wolfgang Hermann?" Anja asked.

"Nothing."

"Blast. All right, keep translating everything we have and see what we can come up with."

Hawk said, "I think the key will be Belgrade. Everything appears to go through there, that much we know. It would seem they have established some kind of distribution network there. We find the hub and we're a long way towards blowing this thing wide apart."

"Would Leonid know?" Ilse asked.

"Maybe. But if he does, he's keeping it to himself. I think he's playing with us. He knew that Dodoma was a Medusa operation. Where are we on discovering the owner of Dittmar Lines?"

Karl shook his head. "The owner is a man who has been dead for five years."

Anja's phone buzzed and she moved away from the group to take the call. While she was tied up, the others discussed options on how to proceed. When she was finished and had rejoined them, they all noticed the puzzled expression on her face.

"What is it, boss?" Hawk asked.

"That was Mary Thurston. We're being recalled to Hereford."

"But what about our mission?" Ilse asked.

"We're to drop it immediately."

"This is starting to sound ominous," Hawk said.

Anja nodded, a grim expression on her face. "Very."

CHAPTER SIX

Hereford, England

"YOU EVER BEEN HERE BEFORE?" Hawk asked Anja as they sat waiting to be summoned.

"No."

"I feel like I'm waiting to be brought before the headmaster."

"You don't have to be here, you know?"

"Yes, I do."

They were both seated in the waiting area of the Global Corporation. Global was a private military contracting firm performing jobs for the government that it couldn't be seen doing for itself, creating plausible deniability. The Corporation was Talon's actual employer.

The sound of high heels on the sterile white tile floor echoed along a hallway announcing the approach of a long-legged woman with dark hair and a short black skirt with matching top.

"Say one word, Jake, and I'll have you cleaning toilets in Iceland," Anja said out of the corner of her mouth.

"Wouldn't dream of it, boss."

The young woman stopped in front of them and said politely, "They will see you now."

They followed her along the hallway to the end before turning right into another. This one led to a large conference room. She held a door open for them to pass through before letting it close behind them.

Inside the conference room was a long wooden table. Seated at it were three people.

Mary Thurston was a former general in her early forties. She was fit and good at her job. Today she wore a pants suit, and her long hair was up in a bun, keeping it formal. Straight away Anja knew this did not bode well.

Hank Jones was another former US general, only at one point in his career, before he came across to run Global, he'd been Chairman of the Joint Chiefs. He was a big, bear of a man who had served in Vietnam as a Special Forces operator.

The third person was George Peacock, the owner and CEO of Global. He, like Hank Jones, was dressed in a suit. The balding man with tired eyes, in another life, had once commanded the British SAS squadrons.

Yes, this wasn't good.

Hawk smiled and Hank Jones's eyes narrowed. "What's he doing here?"

"Moral support," Hawk replied.

"Then you can leave."

Hawk shook his head. "Nope."

The former general's face changed color. "I don't quite think I heard you right, son."

"I'm staying, sir. As man in command of ground operations I have a right to be here. Besides, if this is about some kind of fuckup then it was probably me who caused it."

"Christ."

"Let's get to the point, shall we?" Thurston said, trying to defuse the situation.

"Fine," Jones grunted. "Mister Peacock."

Peacock's face remained passive as he focused his gaze on Anja. "Thank you, General. Miss Meyer, you have been recalled to Hereford because a minister from the British government reached out to me about something troubling."

"Sir?"

"It seems that you are running a current operation with a serving German minister in your sights. Is that correct?"

"Yes, sir. Wolfgang Hermann."

"Then it has to stop."

"The fuck it does," Hawk growled.

All eyes on the opposite side of the table centered on Hawk who was silent once more.

"May I ask, why, sir?" Anja said.

"Because we can't have a covert team conducting an operation against an official of the German government."

"Is that coming from you or from the British government, sir?"

"Both."

"I see."

"I don't," Hawk said.

Jones leaned forward and narrowed his eyes once more. "You've obviously got something to say, son, so have at it."

Hawk glanced at Anja. "Boss?"

She nodded. "By all means, Mister Hawk. Use your usual eloquence."

"My what?" He looked at her incredulously.

"Just tell it how it is." She shook her head with a wry smile.

"Got it." He turned his attention back to the three people waiting on him. There was a slight hint of a smile on Thurston's face as though she knew what was coming. "This is fucking bullshit. Those stupid twats wouldn't know what fucking day of the week it was. As the boss said, I'll tell you how it is, so you understand what life is like on the ground. We received intel that Wolfgang Hermann is operating a trafficking operation out of Tanzania and shipping his product to Belgrade."

"Where did the intel come from?" Peacock asked.

"Leonid Federov."

Jones and Peacock glanced at each other. Thurston on the other hand stared at those opposite. Peacock said, "Wasn't he Viktor Medvedev's righthand man?"

"He was," Anja replied. "We now have him tucked away in a secure facility in Europe where he provides us with actionable intel. So far, he has done rather well."

Jones looked at Thurston. "Mary?"

"Yes?"

"You knew about this?"

She nodded. "I did."

"And you forgot to mention it?"

"No. Chose not to would be a better choice of words."

"Shit."

"Not the point," Hawk said. "The Tanzania part of the operation is—or was—run by Medusa, specifically designed to provide Hermann with what he needed."

"Which is what?" Peacock asked.

"Black people," Anja answered. "Not just women. They took men and children as well. It's like modern day slavery."

When she had come for the meeting, Anja had brought with her the ledger and the coded diary found in Dar es Salaam. She put them on the table. "These are what we found at the offices of the Dittmar Lines shipping company in Dar es Salaam. It doesn't take a genius to link the codes to what is in the ledger."

"And Hermann is linked to this shipping company?" Jones asked.

"The connection is there. We just have to find it."

"Then until you do, you must stand down."

"How are we meant to find a connection if we have to stand down?"

"I can't help you with that, I'm afraid."

Hawk could see Anja's ire rising before his eyes and he knew of only one way to defuse the problem. "Request permission to take R&R?"

She looked at him in disbelief. "What?"

"I'm requesting permission to take R&R," he repeated.

"Permission granted," Thurston said before Anja could speak.

"We're in the middle of something, Jake," Anja scolded him.

"Not according to the head shed. So I figured it would be an opportune time to take a few days off."

"How long, Mister Hawk?" Thurston asked.

"Maybe a week, ma'am."

"I think we can manage that. I'm sure the rest of the team will be looking to enjoy some downtime. Right, Anja?"

"If you insist."

Peacock and Jones stood up. The Global owner said, "That went better than expected. I'll let Downing Street know that it has all been taken care of. Hank, walk with me, I would like to discuss some other things with you if you have the time?"

"Yes, sir."

As the big man walked past Hawk he glared in his direction. The former SAS operator smiled. "Good to see you, sir. You, too, Colonel."

"Stay out of trouble, Mister Hawk."

"You know me, sir."

"Yes, like Raymond Jensen. Two of my best, brightest, and biggest pains in the ass I could ever wish for."

The two men disappeared, and Anja whirled on Hawk. "What the hell was that?"

He held up both of his hands in a defensive position.

"Easy, boss, it's not what you think. General, do you think they bought it?"

Thurston shook her head. "Not in the slightest, Jake."

"Bought what?" Anja asked.

"My R&R plan."

"R&R? Where the hell are you going to go on R&R?"

"Belgrade."

"Not on your own you're not," Anja stated. "Take Ilse with you. Or Gray."

There was a knock on the door and when it opened Karl poked his head around the corner. "Am I too late?"

"What is it, Karl?" Anja asked in exasperation.

"I found something while I was digging into Hermann's background." He glanced warily at Thurston.

"It's all right, Karl. I'm friendly today."

"What is it, Karl?"

He came into the conference room and closed the door. Tucked under his arm he had a folder. Before he went any further however he reached into his pocket for a small bottle of hand sanitizer he kept there.

"Why don't you wear gloves, Karl?" Hawk asked.

He heard Anja give a grumpy sigh. Turning to her he said, "It was a genuine question. I want to know why? It would be easier."

"I have trouble with it."

Hawk nodded, accepting the explanation. "OK."

Thurston said, "Karl, how long since you've talked to someone about it?"

"It's been a while, ma'am."

"If you think it will help, we have a great psychologist here you could talk with."

"I'll think about it."

"That's fine, no pressure. Now, what did you find?"

"A name. Jonas Sauer."

"Who is Jonas Sauer?"

"Back in the nineties Jonas Sauer tried to break into

70

German politics by forming his own party. The One Race Party. They were a bunch of Neo Nazis who wanted Germany to remain white and—well, you know how it goes."

Anja nodded. "Go on."

"When everything blew up in his face after it started riots and all kinds of civil unrest, Jonas Sauer disappeared off the radar. No one knew what happened to him. Until now."

Hawk rolled his eyes. "Come on, Karl, the suspense is killing us."

"More to the point," Anja said, "how did you come up with Jonas Sauer?"

"One of the shell companies I came across was called Sauer Enterprises. So, as they say, I went down that rabbit hole and came up with Jonas Sauer. Only because he and Hermann have one thing in common."

"The race thing?" Hawk asked.

"Yes." Karl opened the folder he had with him and took out two pictures. He placed them side by side and said, "Here I have a picture of Sauer and the other is Hermann. Look at them and tell me what you see."

They looked at the pictures. One was that taken years before of a man in his early forties. The other was of Hermann, gray-haired and looking his seventy-years. Hawk said, "A younger man and an old crook."

"Now look at them closer."

They all stared at the photos in silence.

———

"I'VE GOT IT," Jake said. "The marks on their necks. Are they birthmarks or something?"

Karl nodded. "That's right. Birthmarks."

He took out two more pictures from his folder and lay them out. They were taken and blown up from the pictures already on the table. "Look at the marks," Karl said. "They are identical."

"He's right," agreed Anja. "But he doesn't look like Sauer."

"Plastic surgery," Karl said. He took out some printed documents. "I found these made out from a plastic surgeon in Amsterdam. Don't ask me how I found them, I have no idea. They are made out to Jonas Sauer. I'm guessing after that he changed his name."

"So, we've got the current German Defense minister who was once a radical Neo-Nazi and is now one of the largest traffickers of black people on the planet," Thurston said.

"It would explain why we've been warned off him," Anja said. "That would be the last thing anyone would want to come out. Who was it that reached out to the government?"

Thurston frowned. "I don't know, I wasn't told. Can I get a copy of what you have, Karl? I'll take it to Hank Jones. In the meantime—"

"I'm going to Belgrade," Hawk said. "Alone."

Belgrade, Serbia

"Mister and Mrs. Hawk. We have a booking for the honeymoon suite."

Ilse hit him in the ribs with her elbow, the rock-hard muscle she found taking the blow.

"I can't see it, sir," the young desk clerk responded with a frown.

"Are you su—" He grunted as Ilse hit him.

"The booking is under the name Walker. There are two rooms," Ilse explained.

The clerk smiled. "Oh, yes, here it is. Is there much baggage?"

"Just a couple of cases," Ilse replied, indicating the suitcases behind them.

"I'll have the porter bring them up."

"Don't bother. My friend here can carry them."

Hawk pulled a face behind her back. The clerk tried to stifle a grin and said, "It's no trouble. They will be up shortly."

"Thank you."

She handed the two keycards over to Ilse and said, "Rooms four-oh-five and six."

They climbed into the elevator and Hawk pressed the button for floor four. He turned and looked at Ilse. She glared at him. "Don't you ever grow up?"

Hawk shrugged. "I stare at death most days. That's about all the growing up I can handle."

The elevator dinged and the doors slid open. They stepped out into the hallway and went to the right. Towards the end of the hallway was where they found the two rooms. Side-by-side.

"Which one do you want?" Hawk asked Ilse.

She pointed ay the second of the two. "This one will do. I'm going to have a shower and then we'll meet downstairs in the bar for a drink?"

"In an hour?"

"Sure."

A shower sounded good to Hawk, and he took off his clothes almost immediately. He then went into the bathroom but before he could turn the water on there was a knock at the door. Hawk muttered a curse but then remembered he was waiting on his baggage. One measly bag.

He wrapped a towel around himself and walked out to the door. He opened it and was surprised to see the clerk and the porter there together. She looked surprised to be greeted by the half-naked operative, and after she'd gathered herself, she said, "We have your bag, Mister…Walker?"

She let her brown eyes wander over his torso, taking in all of his contours as well as the scars. Hawk took the bag from the porter who left immediately. "Call me Jake," Hawk said.

"Uh, huh."

"Um, I was just about to have a shower."

"Don't let me keep you, sir."

Hawk closed the door and went back into the bathroom after dumping the bag on the large bed. He turned the water on making sure that it was nice and hot before climbing in and shutting the door behind him.

To his right was a little shelf with all the usual complimentary items. Shampoo, conditioner, soap. There was one thing there that made him frown. A small square-shaped packet. He picked it up and saw the circular ring shape which was on the inside. "Fuck me, they think of everything."

He sensed her before she stepped into the shower. Even though he was always on edge, expecting the worst, especially in 'enemy territory,' he somehow knew that the presence in the bathroom wasn't a threat. "You could get fired for this," Hawk said.

"I am on my break."

He turned and looked at her. She was naked, her small breasts firm, nipples erect as was her goose bumped skin.

"You'd better close the door."

As she turned to close it, Hawk moved closer, his hands reaching out, touching her pale skin before they moved around to cup her breasts. He pinched her nipples between thumb and forefinger, eliciting a sharp gasp. He felt himself grow hard, pressing against her round buttocks.

She turned back and looked into Hawk's eyes. He smiled at her and said, "I don't even know your name."

She returned his smile as her hand drifted down from his chest to his lower half and said, "No, you don't."

———

THE SEX WAS hard and furious, almost animalistic. At one point, Hawk thought that the shower screen itself might break from the pounding it was getting.

When it was over, they got out of the shower, dried themselves before dressing, and the desk clerk left, red-faced, and exhausted.

Hawk checked his watch and saw that he was late, by twenty minutes. "Shit."

By the time he got downstairs to the bar, Ilse was already on her second drink. She stared at Hawk as he sat in the bar stool and said, "Was she any good?"

Hawk went red. "You heard?"

"The whole fucking hotel heard."

"Then you should already know the answer."

"Who was she?"

"Does it matter?"

"Damn it, Jake. It matters if we're compromised before we even start."

"The desk clerk."

She sighed. "I should have known."

The barman came along and asked Hawk what he wanted to drink. "Scotch, neat."

He walked off and Hawk said, "I can't help it if I have smoldering British charm."

"James Bond you aren't, sunshine."

Hawk nodded across the island bar to the other side where a couple of young ladies sat staring at him. One had long dark hair, the other was blonde. "I don't know, I might be better."

He twiddled his fingers at them.

"Grow up, Jake," Ilse snapped while the two women giggled at him. "Get your head in the game."

The barman brought Hawk's drink and he paid the man. "What do you want to discuss?"

"What are we going to do now that we are here?"

"I have a contact here from my MI6 days who might be able to help. I could reach out to him."

"Do it."

"I'll take a walk when we finish here and see if he still frequents his usual hangouts," Hawk told her.

"Fine, just be careful. Something isn't right."

"You mean like that guy at our six who has been watching us ever since I came in?" Hawk asked.

"Yes." Ilse had noticed him, too. "And the woman beside your two friends across the way."

"Yeah, I tagged that cow, too. She looks so intense she stands out like dog's bollocks."

"Medusa or Hermann's crowd?"

Hawk shrugged. "Let's find out."

Ilse frowned cautiously. "How?"

"Like this," the former SAS man said and got off his stool.

She watched him closely as he walked around the bar. For a moment the two ladies from earlier thought he might be about to join them but were disappointed when he sat next to the other woman.

"Hey, love," he said by way of greeting.

"What do you want?" she asked rudely, her accent heavy.

"I just wanted to ask you a question. Is that all right? Do you mind?"

"Go away."

He leaned in closer and from where she sat, Ilse noticed that the woman tensed.

Hawk said, "Are you Medusa or Hermann?"

The woman remained silent.

"I thought so. You're Medusa. I bet you have a tattoo, too."

"No, they don't use them anymore."

The response was swift, brought on by nerves. Immediately the woman knew she'd said the wrong thing.

"Is that your friend over there?" Hawk asked. "The only reason I'm here talking to you is because I think you're smarter than him. If I was over there I probably would have killed him by now, love."

She remained silent.

"I'll take that as a yes. Now, listen closely. I'm an old hand at this and I play for keeps. So, if you or your friend, or any others for that matter, get in my rearview mirror, I'm going to put you all down for good. Understand?"

More silence.

Hawk got up. "Thank you for your time."

He walked back around and held out his hand for Ilse to take. He said loudly, "Come on, my sweet, our room awaits."

She smiled at him, and they walked hand in hand out of the bar. "What happened?"

"I told her that I didn't like being followed around."

"Did you find out who they are?" Ilse asked.

"Medusa."

"How do they know we're here?"

"Good intel. The sooner we chop the head off the snake, the better."

"Let's hope it's soon.

They went back upstairs to their rooms and right away when Hawk entered his he knew it had been searched. Just one thing was out of place but it was enough. Hawk picked up a small, but solid candlestick holder made from crystal.

Slowly, as though his every movement could be heard, he swept the rooms until he was certain they were clear.

He'd just replaced it when Ilse entered through the still open door. She looked at him with a puzzled expression on his face. "What is it?"

"Someone has been through my things," he told her.

She looked around the room. "How do you know?"

"I just do."

"Did they take anything?"

"Nothing to take."

"I bet I know who was behind it," Ilse said.

Hawk did, too. "My charm must have lured her out into the open."

"I'm sure it was her who did the luring, Jake."

He frowned. "You may be right."

CHAPTER SEVEN

Belgrade, Serbia

HAWK KNEW he was being followed. There were at least two, maybe three. A woman and two men. Not the ones from the hotel though. These ones were different. As he walked beneath the orange street lamps towards the Danube, he checked his watch. It was 11pm.

Ahead of him was an intersection where he turned right. The street led him down to the river where a string of nightclubs were established. But not the kind that the young party goers frequented. These clubs were for the businessman. Married, single, it didn't matter. They supplied their patrons with alcohol, cigars, drugs, and high-class prostitutes.

The type of people who frequented these places were executives, politicians, political ambassadors, top-class lawyers, and anyone else who had money or sophistication. Not someone like Hawk.

The one he chose was called The Danube Palace. The façade spoke of wealth and class. Outside on the door were two large security guards. Both were dressed in suits. They had the look of ex-military stamped all over them and although no weapons were visible, he was certain they were armed.

Hawk knew there was no getting past them, so he never even tried. He looked at the bigger of the two and said, "I'm here to see Dejan Kovac."

The man looked at him and grunted. "Go away."

Hawk shook his head. "It's important. Tell him Jake is here to see him."

"He is busy."

"He'll make time for me. Tell him to get his dick out of this week's prostitute."

"You need to leave."

"Listen, me and Dejan go way back to when he was a colonel in the army. Just give him the option of seeing me or not. That's all I ask."

The man stared longer before saying, "Wait here."

He went inside and left Hawk outside with the other guard. The former SAS man looked at him. "Busy night?"

The man said nothing.

"Anyone famous inside?"

Nothing.

"No? You're a bag of monkeys aren't you?"

Hawk turned and looked around. He picked out his tails almost immediately. One in the shadows of a doorway across the street. Another in an alleyway, the third in the shadows of another building.

The door opened again and the guard appeared. "Come with me."

Hawk followed him inside. Straight away the music could be heard. It wasn't loud, overpowering like most disco clubs. There was a small foyer which opened out into the main area. There were two dancing stages with lounge chairs spaced around them. Most were occupied as were the stages. Two young ladies danced seductively, net tops to cover their pert breasts and panties which covered nothing much at all.

The crowd was a mix of men and women. Both being attended to by waitresses in more ways than one.

Hawk was led to a cubicle at the back of the room where a balding man in a suit looked up from what he was doing and stared at the former SAS operator. "Jacob Hawk," he said with a thick accent. "It has been a while, my friend."

He was flanked by two women, both tastefully dressed in long, tight-fitting dresses, hair flowing down past their shoulders. Hawk glanced at them.

"You want one?"

Hawk shook his head.

"Both? I let you have a couple of hours with both of them. Anything for my good friend Jake."

Hawk shook his head again. "I need to discuss something with you, Dejan."

The man frowned. "You look so serious, Jake. Sit, have a beer."

The Talon man sat down and one of the ladies moved closer to him. Her perfume was sweet, not pungent and overpowering like many he'd smelled before. He felt her hand lightly touch his thigh as she smiled warmly. "I am Ana."

Hawk smiled. "That's nice."

"I am."

"Easy, Ana. Save it for later," Kovac said.

She leaned back, dragging her hand across Hawk's crotch, giving it a gentle squeeze, eliciting a reaction. Her smile became seductive, and she said, "Yes, later."

"What can I do for you, Jake?"

A beer appeared and was sat in front of Hawk. He stared at it and said, "I need to talk to you about girls."

Kovac raised his eyebrows. "Girls? A man like yourself comes to me about girls?"

Hawk looked around the room and saw movement

near the entrance as three people entered. "A special type of girl, Dejan."

"Go on."

"Black. African. Slaves."

"You will find none of that here, my friend," Kovac said almost indignantly. "Look around you."

"I never said you did, Dejan."

"Then why bring it up?"

"Because somebody here in Belgrade is doing it. Have you heard of Medusa?"

"Who hasn't?"

"Have you ever got girls from them?" Hawk asked.

"Never."

"Can you tell me who?"

Kovac opened his mouth to speak, paused, then, "Not here. Ana, take Jake to the VIP room. I will be there in a little while. Give him whatever he wants."

She smiled broadly. "With pleasure."

"Is that all right, Jake?"

Hawk nodded. "Sure."

Hawk got up from the cubicle seat on which they sat. Ana followed him and took him by the hand. She leaned in close and whispered in his ear, "Follow me."

As they walked through the seats Hawk glanced over his shoulder. He caught sight of Kovac walking towards the bar where one of the three who had recently entered was now standing.

A tug on his hand drew his attention back to Ana. "Are you coming?"

"I guess so."

———

THE VIP ROOM had plush carpet, a large lounge which looked as though it doubled as a makeshift bed, a fridge with alcohol, a bar, a television, and a camera.

"Would you like another drink, Jake. A scotch, perhaps?"

"Sure, why not."

She poured him a drink and passed it to him. She led Hawk to the lounge and sat him down. Hawk took a drink and was about to take another when Ana took it from him. "Finish later."

Ana stood before him and slid her dress from her shoulders, letting it fall to the floor, revealing firm breasts and a black G-string.

Hawk let his gaze wander over her, taking in all he could see. She was a beautiful woman without doubt, and the Talon man could feel himself start to respond.

Ana bent forward and straddled Hawk's thighs. Her lips touched his gently before parting, her tongue flicking like a serpent's between them. Hawk's right hand slid up her slight framed torso and cupped a breast. He squeezed it before pinching an erect nipple between thumb and forefinger. Ana gasped before her movements became more urgent. Her fingers grabbed at Hawk's shirt but before she could go any further, Hawk used his overpowering strength to throw her onto her back.

Ana yelped, her gaze uncertain as she stared up at him. Hawk smiled disarmingly and brought a throaty giggle from Ana who opened her mouth, coaxing him down.

Hawk did as she wished, kissing her again. His right hand slid up across her breasts to her throat, wrapping around it easily.

Then it closed hard.

Ana's eyes bulged with fear as she tried to comprehend what was happening. Above her Hawk's face had changed, a snarling rage evident, fire in his eyes. "Wrap your legs around me," he hissed in a low voice.

She clawed at his hand.

"Do it. For the camera."

Ana's legs came up so it looked as though they were in the throes of passion.

"What is he fucking up to?" Hawk snarled.

Ana struggled against him as she tried to prize his grip away from her throat. "Dejan is up to something, what is it?"

Her reply was a choking gurgle and Hawk released his grasp enough to let some air in. Ana coughed as she gulped in the breaths. "What are you doing?" she asked weakly.

"Dejan has done nothing but lie to me since I've arrived." He slapped her stomach with an open hand. "He told me he'd never done business with Medusa but you have the tattoo. Where are you from?"

"Let me go...please."

"Start talking or I'll break you fucking neck."

"Moldova. I'm from Moldova."

"Is that where they took you from?" Hawk hissed into her ear.

"Yes."

"When?"

"Two years ago."

"Do you want to get out?"

She gave him a confused look.

"Answer the question."

"Y—yes."

"Then tell me what I want to know, and I will help you," Hawk told her.

"How? How can you help me?"

"Well, if this goes how I expect it to, I'm going to have to kill my friend." Hawk let her go and got off her. "Get dressed."

Ana put her dress on and sat on the lounge. While she did that, Hawk took out his cell, dialed, waited for it to be answered, and said, "Bravo One is Code Six." Then Hawk disconnected.

Once Ana was done, Hawk got up, walked over to the corner where the camera sat on the wall in the corner. He reached up and ripped it free, then he waited.

———

WHEN THE DOOR OPENED, Hawk was already in position. The first thing through the door was a fist full of Glock. The Talon operative clamped his left hand down on the wrist and his right hand grasped the handgun. He twisted it savagely, hearing bones break as he did it. He ripped the weapon free of the limp hand, reversed it, and pulled the trigger.

BANG! BANG!

The man on the receiving end of the shots stopped screaming as both rounds punched into his chest, forcing the air out of his lungs, leaving him opening and closing his mouth like a fish.

Hawk ignored him; he was out of the fight. The next threat was behind the first now. Another shooter, his weapon up, and ready to fire.

Hawk ducked back just as he squeezed the trigger. The bullet burned past his head as he ducked out of the way behind the door. Anticipating the shooter would enter the room after the shot, the Talon operator fired three shots through the hollow-core door.

Three holes appeared while on the other side, the exit holes splintered wide as the rounds punched violently through. A loud cry filled the room and the man staggered forward, a deep red hole in the side of his face, razor sharp splinters forming a pattern around it.

Hawk stepped forward, and with the gun no more than a foot from the man's head, fired, painting the wall opposite with bright red blood.

The Talon man checked the open doorway to see if there were any more threats. It was clear and he knelt beside the first man, now dead, to check for spare magazines.

Movement almost startled him from the open door. The Glock in his hand came up and aimed center mass at the woman facing him with her own weapon. These were the three who'd been following him.

Both of them stared at one another, their fingers resting on the triggers, ready to fire. Hawk said, "Medusa? You here with Balzer?"

The woman remained silent, her aim unwavering, her blue-eyed stare, unblinking. Kovac appeared behind her, behind him, two more men. He took in the situation and then looked back to his former friend. "Jake, what have you done?"

"What the fuck have *you* done, Dejan? You let these pricks try to kill me. Set me fucking up for them."

"It is not what you think."

The woman started to step into the room. Hawk moved backward and soon they were all inside, Ana huddled on the lounge, petrified of what might happen next.

"What a mess," Kovac whined.

"You caused it. All I wanted was some answers."

"I gave them to you."

"You gave me lies, Dejan. Then fucking set me up." Using his free hand, Hawk pointed at Ana. "She came from Medusa. She has the tattoo."

"So I may have bought some girls from them. What of it?"

Hawk shook his head. "You're just as bad as them, Dejan."

The Serbian shrugged. "What do we do now, Jake?"

"I'm going to leave here with the girl."

Kovac's eyes hardened. "No, the woman stays. She cost me two hundred thousand. She goes nowhere."

Hawk looked at the woman pointing the gun at him.

"Are you going to put that thing down or am I going to have to shoot you?"

Nothing.

"Shit." He didn't want to kill her but she was stuffing everything up. If he didn't get out soon the police would be there and he'd be deeper in the shit. So he adjusted his aim ever so slightly and before the woman knew what had happened, he'd fired.

The bullet ripped into her arm but instead of going through it, the slug ran up it destroying tissue and bone as it went.

She cried out, the gun she held falling from lifeless fingers to the floor with a dull thud. Hawk then changed his aim again, this time putting down both of Kovac's guards with bullets to the chest.

Then he pointed the gun at Kovac and said, "I'm disappointed, Dejan. I thought we were friends."

The club owner held out a hand. "Don't shoot me, Jake."

Beside Hawk on the floor, the wounded woman moved to get her weapon, struggling but winning the fight against the excruciating pain ripping through the limb. "You're a persistent cow," Hawk snapped at her.

He kicked the weapon across the room. "Back door, Dejan?'

He pointed over his shoulder. "Out there, to the left."

Hawk stepped forward and pressed the Glock against his former friend's head.

"No!"

"If you or any of your people try to come after me, I'll come back and punch your ticket, cock. Understood?"

"Yes.

The handgun rose and fell, knocking the Serbian out. Hawk turned to Ana. "Come on unless you're staying."

She got to her feet, a trembling hand going to her mouth as she looked around. "What have you done?"

87

"What I needed to. Now, move."

Hawk led her out through the back of the club which opened out onto a boardwalk along the river away from the deck where partygoers frequented.

Moments later they were both out the front. A large crowd which had been inside milled around after fleeing the gunshots. In the distance Hawk heard the sirens.

"This way," he said as they started walking along the narrow street.

A roar and suddenly a van pulled up beside them. The window came down and Ilse said, "Get in."

CHAPTER EIGHT

"MI6 HAVE SET us up with a safehouse," Ilse said as she changed gears and turned right into a narrow street. "I made some calls after our rooms were compromised."

"Handy to know people," Hawk said.

"What happened?"

"My friend was in bed with some not so friendly people. Medusa."

"Is Balzer here?"

"I don't know. We have to assume he is."

"I'll let—"

"No one know," Hawk finished for her. "We're not here."

"Don't be daft, Jake. Everyone knows we're fucking here," Ilse snapped. "But right now we have to work out what to do with the girl."

"Take her to the British embassy. Since everyone knows we're here, tell the boss and let her sort the shit out."

"Why so angry, Jake?" Ilse asked. "I'm not the enemy."

"I'm bloody angry because I should have shot my old friend. I've a feeling it's going to come back and haunt us."

"I don't want to—"

"You're bloody going," Hawk snapped, cutting Ana off. "If you ever want to see Moldova again it's the best place for you."

They drove in silence for a while, every now and then passing a police vehicle as it headed towards the river.

Hawk eventually reached into his pocket and took out his encrypted cell. He dialed a number and heard Anja's accented voice say, "What have you done, Jake?"

"Why do I have to have done something?"

"Because it's almost midnight and you are calling me from Belgrade where you are holidaying."

"Yeah, well, the holiday isn't going so well."

"Do tell."

He filled her in on the recent events. When he was finished she asked him two questions. "Is Balzer there?"

"It is a possibility."

"What do you want me to do about the girl?"

"We're taking her to the British embassy."

"I'll see what I can do."

"Thank you."

"Am I going to see your face all over Interpol wanted posters, Jake?" Anja asked.

"Only the ones they put me on, boss."

She sighed. "Leave it with me."

"Yes, ma'am."

The call disconnected and he put the cell away. He sat there silently until Ilse asked, "How did that go?"

"Oddly well."

"She's probably waiting to see you face to face."

"That's what worries me," Hawk replied. He turned to Ana. "I never got to ask Dejan what I wanted to know, so I'll ask you. Somewhere in Belgrade a club is operating which caters only black girls. Where?"

Even though he couldn't see her face too well, he sensed her body tense. "I—I'm not sure."

"Don't lie to me Ana. Now is not the time."

There was a long pause before she said, "There is a place. North of the city. An estate. It is called a hotel, but it is not. Men and women come to stay there but not for holiday."

"What is the name of it?" Hawk asked.

"Amsel Haus," she replied.

"How do I know what you're telling me is true?" Hawk asked her.

"It's true," Ilse said over her shoulder. "It's German. Translated it says Blackbird House."

"Tell me all you know," Hawk said to Ana.

"It is run by a terrible woman. It is said that if Satan had a daughter, she would be it. It is also said that if she becomes displeased with those that work for her, they are sent to Yazikstan."

Hawk had heard of Yazikstan. It was a hot bed of terrorist camps in Eastern Europe protected by the dictator government, armed by Russia who fed it with oil and gas. It had once been a province of Kazakhstan but had broken away from the country to become realigned with the mother country.

Already knowing the answer, Hawk asked, "What's in Yazikstan?"

"They are sent to the camps."

He knew what she meant. They were sent to the terrorist training camps where they would be given as wives to those not left long for the world. It would be a brutal existence because once their husbands were gone they would be married off to others or cast aside to live or die on their own.

"What is the woman's name?" Hawk asked.

"Natalija Novak."

"What else do you know about her?"

"It is said that she was once in the military. She was kicked out because she was caught sleeping with her troops. The female ones."

"Okay. So she likes taking the field with her own side."

"Not just that, only the black ones."

Hawk was confused. "She hates them but sleeps with them. Is that right?"

"Yes. She likes the power it gives her."

"Psycho bitch."

The cell in Hawk's pocket buzzed. He took it out and frowned. No ID. Curiously he hit the answer button and said, "Yeah?"

"Hello, Jake?"

"Who the fuck is this?"

"I think you already know."

"Balzer?"

"That's right," came the reply.

"What the fuck do you want?"

"For you to go away."

Hawk tutted him. "Can't do that."

"I thought so. Never mind. I'll make sure to send flowers to Anja for your funeral."

Hawk opened his mouth to reply but the words never got past his lips. Ilse's cry of alarm saw to that.

"*Jake!*"

Suddenly the world reeled violently and for a moment everything went black.

———

"COME ON, Jake, wake up. I don't have time for this shit."

His eyes came open with a start. "What shitting happened?"

"The bastards hit us with a truck."

"Are you alright?" he asked, trying to sit up.

"I'm fine. A bit banged up."

"Am I alright?"

92

"Are you?"

"Where's my gun?" he asked, patting himself down, the anger within him rising.

She shoved an M6A2 carbine in his hands. "Go get them, Tiger."

"Where are they?" Bullets started punching into the van, opening holes like a can opener. "Forget I fucking asked. Get the girl out."

"She's dead. The truck hit her side."

"Motherfucker," Hawk growled and kicked the rear doors of the van.

When only one flew open, he realized they were on their side. "If this shit was in a book no one would believe it."

Bolts of pain shot through his body as he moved. Soon he was outside and using the van for cover. Seconds later, as he started firing, Ilse joined him. It was then he realized she was actually hurt worse than she let on. "Get down, girl," he ordered, firing at a shooter using a streetlamp for cover.

"I'm fine."

"You can hardly walk."

"I can still shoot," she retorted and to prove her point, she opened fire, putting down the man targeted by Hawk.

"I guess you can," he said. "Cover this corner."

He moved along the side of the van to the back end which he peered around. Four more shooters. He changed hands and brought the M6 up. The red dot of the sights settled on the first shooter, and he squeezed the trigger.

The carbine rattled and the man was flung onto his back as the rounds hammered into his chest.

Hawk pulled back as bullets peppered the van on his corner. He waited for a lull and repeated his last movements. This time, however, he missed.

He was about to fire again when headlights lit him up like a bomber caught in searchlights over Germany in

1944. He held up his hand against the glare as it slid to a halt and the doors flung open.

His M6 came up and across. "X-Rays to our rear!" he cried out and opened fire with the weapon on full auto, bullets smashing the headlights.

To Hawk's left, Ilse dropped to her knee and opened fire at the vehicle door where one of the new threats was sheltered. She squeezed the trigger and the window in the door shattered before the man behind it jerked wildly and fell to the damp street.

"Watch your corner!" Hawk shouted and started to walk towards the newly arrived vehicle.

As bullets cracked around him, the Talon operative told himself to remain calm and pick his targets as he pressed forward.

Another shooter fell, leaving two still standing. Hawk targeted the one on the right. The M6 rattled loudly in his hands as the 5.56 rounds spewed forward. The Talon operative heard the man cry out and he disappeared behind the vehicle. Hawk changed targets sweeping the M6 to the left and letting the red dot sight settle on the remaining shooter. He squeezed the trigger.

One shot sounded; that was all he had left in the magazine. "Christ," he growled, throwing the carbine aside.

Running forward, he put the vehicle between himself and the remaining shooter. He dived down, rolled, grabbed a dead man's weapon, came up, and opened fire in one smooth movement.

Instead of shooting across the roof of the vehicle, he shot through it, the rounds punching into the shocked Medusa shooter. The man shouted and dropped to his knees. Hawk fired another two rounds that drilled into the man's head, killing him.

The Talon operative came to his feet. "Fucking asshole," he cursed, shaking his head as he walked steadily back towards the van, only pausing to pick up the M6.

Hawk dropped out the spent magazine and then shouted to Ilse, "Where's the spare ammo?"

"In the van."

Bullets hammered the destroyed vehicle and Hawk ducked down. "They bloody would be."

Once more, the M6 clattered to the asphalt. He looked over the foreign weapon that he'd picked up. It was an AK-12. Hawk checked the banana magazine and found it to be about half full.

"I'm out!" Ilse called out. She tossed her M6 on the ground at her feet.

A grim expression came over Hawk's face. He nodded towards the shooter's vehicle at their rear and said, "Get back there. You'll find some weapons. I'll be right behind you."

Lifting the AK-12, he aimed it around the corner of the van, firing at the remaining shooters. The exchange of fire intensified as Ilse hobbled head down, flat out towards the other vehicle.

Soon the AK-12 was empty, and out of habit, Hawk took out the magazine, looked at it, and then threw it on the ground, followed by the weapon. Suddenly everything went quiet. And, through the deafening silence, a voice rang out. "Are you still alive, Jake?"

"You better believe it, mate. Take a lot more than your pussy whipped cocks to kill me."

"I see you have a sense of humor. We'll see if you're still laughing as you're bleeding out in the gutter."

"Ha-ha. Suck my dick."

Hawk looked at the gap between himself and the other vehicle. For at least part of the journey, he would be out in the open. But he could rely on Ilse to try and cover him as he ran.

"You ready, my love?" he called out.

"Don't you ever call me that again," Ilse shot back

at him.

Hawk grinned. He had to give her one thing, she was cool in a crisis. "On my way."

The Talon operative broke cover running as fast as he could, pain from the crash still tearing through his bruised muscles. He reached the vehicle and crouched down beside Ilse. "Are you OK?"

"I'll live."

Hawk found himself another weapon. It, too, was an AK-12. He checked the magazine and slotted it back home before grabbing two more fully loaded mags from the webbing of a dead shooter. He passed one to Ilse. "Here, take that."

Bullets pounded the vehicle providing sanctuary. The shooters had shifted and now they were using the wrecked van for cover. Ilse looked at Hawk and asked, "What do you propose to do now, Monty?"

He stared at her. "Really? You want to use comedy now."

"It takes my mind off dying. Especially with you. Crazy asshole."

"I'm a crazy asshole? I—"

WHAP!

Ilse's jaw dropped open, and she sank to the ground. Hawk stared at her, stunned by what had just happened. Then realization set in. "No! No! No!"

He lurched to her side. Even under the orange street-lamps he could already see the bloodstain starting to spread. He pressed hard on the wound. "Don't you fucking die on me now." His words were merely pleas. He'd seen comrades die from wounds like this one. High up to the left.

Ilse's eyes were wide, her mouth working as she tried to fill her lungs with the next gasp of breath. "J—Jake?"

"Don't talk, love. Just stay awake. You'll be fine."

"Is—is it b—bad?"

"No. We'll get you to a hospital and get you fixed up."

There were bubbles of air coming from the wound and he knew he needed to plug it. He ripped some fabric from her shirt. "Sorry, this is going to hurt."

Brutally he forced the scrap of cotton into the hole, plugging it as best he could. Ilse arched her back, crying out as pain tore through her chest. "That'll hold for the moment."

"I—I can't breathe."

He looked at the wound. Her chest cavity was filling with blood. "It's all good," he lied.

Bullets hammered the vehicle. He glanced up and saw the shooters advancing. He hissed angrily. "I'll be right back, baby."

"D—don't leave me, J—Jake. I—I can't—can't breathe."

"Sorry," he replied and came to his feet.

The AK-12 in his hands rattled to life as he started to mow down the men coming towards him. Anger surged through his soul as he became oblivious to the danger presented to his safety. Killing all those before him became his ultimate goal. Somehow the shooters had multiplied. Maybe they'd been reinforced by another vehicle, but those coming towards him now numbered six.

Not for long because two were down and one was falling. Three still shooting. Hawk ground his teeth, taking a deep breath as he emptied the magazine. He dropped out the empty and replaced it.

That left two.

Most likely it was dumb luck that Hawk was even still alive. Or maybe he'd put them on the back foot with his brazen assault. Either way, he was still upright and untouched.

The AK-12 spoke again, and another man was down.

Hawk felt the rage still building inside start to spill over. With an angry growl which exploded from his lips he put the final shooter down.

Before walking away from them Hawk shot every single one of them again, making sure they were staying there, not getting up to be a threat. Only then did he turn around and hurry back to where Ilse lay prone.

He knelt beside her. She was unresponsive. Her face in the orange light, a different color. She stopped breathing. "Come on, girl, don't do this to me. Not now."

His time in special forces had served him well. Throughout all the intense training that the men received, one course stood out above all else. Each man was trained to triage on the battlefield.

There wasn't any time to lose. He lurched sideways to where one of the dead shooters lay. He patted him down and found what he was looking for. A short, bladed combat knife.

His fingers kept exploring the dead man, until by luck, he found something else. A pen. He unscrewed it, took the guts out of it before screwing it back together. Then he knelt beside Ilse, cut her clothing away to expose her chest. Then he ran his fingers down her exposed side, feeling the ribs as he went.

He said through gritted teeth, "Sorry about this, but that's what they make antibiotics for."

Hawk inserted the knife between her ribs, warm blood spurting as he did so. He withdrew it and then grabbed the pen carcass. Prying the wound open with his fingers, he inserted the pen until he heard the rush of air.

Suddenly Ilse convulsed and drew gulps of air into her lungs. "Good girl, welcome back."

Ilse coughed.

"Just take it easy, we'll have you patched up in no time."

The night rang out with the sound of approaching sirens. Hawk reached into his pocket and took out his cell. He dialed and waited for the voice on the other end.

"Yeah, the holiday is fucked."

CHAPTER NINE

Belgrade, Serbia

MARY THURSTON and Anja sat down opposite Hawk in the interview room. It had taken them 24 hours, but they had finally arrived. "How is she?" he asked, staring at Anja.

Her reply was, "Stable. Lost a lot of blood but the doctor said what you did most likely saved her life."

"Good."

"No, not good," Thurston said. "This whole thing has turned into a shit show. Bodies everywhere, dead, wounded. This was meant to be a sneak and peek. The authorities want to throw the book at you. You'll be lucky to see sunlight ever again."

"Don't bet on it."

"This is not a damn game, Jake."

"Too fucking right it isn't. I had a friend set me up to be killed, another almost died, and the lass we rescued is in a body bag. You don't see me bloody laughing about that. I'm pissed off and this doesn't end until the last bastard goes down."

"It's over, Jake," Anja said. "The corporation has

managed to pull a few strings to get you released but only if you are taken out of the country never to return."

"This isn't over, boss."

"It is as far as you are concerned."

"But I found out where the hub of the operation is."

"You'll have to be satisfied with Balzer," Anja said.

"I got him?"

She nodded.

"I'm sorry."

Anja frowned. "What for?"

"Because he was your friend."

"That friend died a long time ago. With him gone, Medusa's operation in Africa transporting sex slaves now has a hole in it."

Hawk's face took on a grim expression. "Not for long, Noskov will have someone fill it without raising a sweat."

"Then we'll change our focus and concentrate on finding him."

Hawk was frustrated. "Who is watching Ilse?"

"Gray."

"Are you all right, Jacob?" Anja asked. "You look a little worse for wear."

"Getting in a crash will do that to you. I'm a bit stiff but otherwise fine."

"Stay that way. You'll be out of here in a couple of hours," she said, standing up. "Just keep out of trouble."

When they departed, Hawk was handcuffed and taken from the room. He was escorted down a hallway, past the holding cell where he'd been held, and out into a sun filled yard surrounded by solid concrete block walls topped with razor wire. The guard turned to leave.

"Hey, Boris, what's going on?"

"Exercise," the man grunted.

Hawk watched him go before looking around the enclosure once more. That was when he noticed a total absence of cameras. There had been some at one point but they had been removed. Violently.

The door opened and Hawk turned to look. Two men walked through the opening. Big, hulking brutes, their faces set in what appeared to be permanent scowls. Both were Hawk's size if a little wider. One had a goatee beard, both had tattoos. He looked at them, noticing the swastikas first. One also had a Parteiadler tattooed on a thick arm while the other sported a lightning bolt SS brand.

Neo Nazis. Things just got worse.

They walked into the yard slowly before starting to circle the Talon operative. Hawk instantly became all too aware that his hands were still cuffed, and these guys weren't.

"Nice day," Hawk said.

"For some of us," the first of the two said. He had a heavy accent.

"Let me guess. You're German, right?"

"You don't like Germans?"

"Nothing against them, personally," Hawk allowed.

They kept circling him for a minute longer before they both stopped. The man who spoke reached behind his back and pulled out a shiv made from what looked to be a spoon. He grinned wickedly at Hawk as his friend did the same.

The Talon operative's senses heightened exponentially as he tried to figure out a way to take on both of the killers without getting killed himself.

With nothing better in his arsenal, he settled on his British wit. "You cocks have got fucking shit tattoos."

All the amusement was gone now. The first man closed in on Hawk who had taken a few steps back before he stopped. The attacker lunged and Hawk jumped to the left extending his cuffed wrists and catching the knife wrist neatly between cuffs and short chain.

He then turned so that the attacker's arm came up over his shoulder before violently wrenching it down with brutal force.

Hawk heard the bones snap sickeningly, followed by a high-pitched shriek of pain.

The Talon operative turned back, releasing the damaged arm. The shiv had dropped from the man's hand and clinked on the concrete at Hawk's feet. He dropped down, sweeping it up in his right hand, the cuffs making the move awkward.

But he succeeded anyway. The pointy end, sharp, deadly, came sweeping up and drove upward under the killer's chin, through flesh, pinned the tongue to the roof of his mouth then continued into the brain.

The man dropped like a marionette with its strings cut, body quivering.

Hawk turned to face his friend. "Your turn, mate. I hope you've made peace with whoever it is you pray to."

There was uncertainty in the second man's eyes as he stared at his dead friend. The uncertainty was rapidly replaced by anger as he let the emotion engulf him. He charged at Hawk like some wild beast, fire in its eyes.

The charge was easily sidestepped and as the man went past, Hawk's foot lashed out, tripping him as he went.

The man stumbled and crashed forward, his head smashing into the blockwork of the wall with a wet smack. Hawk winced. "Bet that hurt."

He waited, expecting the man to climb to his feet. Instead, the body remained immobile. Hawk walked over and looked down, noting the eyes were open but staring vacantly.

"Nope, never felt a thing."

Then the Talon operator sat down to wait.

———

HE DIDN'T HAVE to wait long. The door opened once more, and a woman walked through escorted by two tall broad-shouldered men. Her dark hair was cut short in a bob. The dress she had on beneath an open, knee-length coat was black and white, the plunging neckline exposing just enough cleavage to avoid looking slutty. She smiled at Hawk and said, "You are very good, Mister Hawk. I can see why my employer is so concerned about you."

"Which one is that?" Hawk asked as he came to his feet.

"I'm sure you know Ilya."

"We've crossed paths. Are you here to finish what your tossers couldn't?"

"That was the plan."

"But?"

"After seeing you in action, I think there might be another use for you. If you are open to offers?"

"Are you part of the offer?" Hawk asked, raising an eyebrow.

She smiled seductively. "I am a sophisticated woman, Mister Hawk, not a slut you can pick up, fuck, and then discard."

"Do I at least get a name?" She had an accent he couldn't quite place.

"I am Desarae."

"The one desired by everyone," Hawk said with a wide grin.

"I'm impressed. You are not just a brute." She lifted a manicured index finger to her jawline as though deep in thought.

Hawk indicated the two dead men. "I try to fit both shoes. You're Medusa?"

The woman chuckled. "Medusa, Medusa, Medusa. The organization is fractured. It has been from the moment Ilya murdered Viktor Medvedev. One decent blow and it will shatter completely."

"What kind of blow?" Hawk asked.

"One from the top."

The Talon operative nodded. "It's a cutthroat world you people operate in. But tell me, why do you want to knock your boss off if it will shatter the empire?"

She opened her mouth to speak.

"Wait, don't tell me, you want to be there to pick up the pieces?"

"Only the important ones. No one person should wield that much power."

Hawk nodded thoughtfully. "And how do you propose to do this?"

Desarae smiled, her red lipstick stark against pearly white teeth.

"You want me to do it? Of course, you do. Why me?"

"Because of the way you dealt with Rolf and his people."

It was Hawk's turn to chuckle. "I already have a job."

She walked towards him, stopping close before leaning in to whisper, "I will pay you more."

He could smell the sweet scent of her perfume. "How much more?" he asked, his voice husky with feigned desire.

Desarae stepped back, her eyes sparkling. "Five million."

"That's a lot of money."

"It's a lot of job."

"How do you expect me to do it?"

"You will need to draw him out of hiding," Desarae said.

"How?"

"I know why you are here. I have a team in place to stop you. If you succeed in your task, it might bring Ilya from hiding."

"You mean shut down Hermann's operation?"

Desarae smiled. "Yes."

"But we're going to do that anyway, so why should I work for you?"

"Because you will die right here and now if you refuse. My way, you get to live, and you get paid as well."

He looked at her thoughtfully.

The woman gave a bored sigh. "And don't even think you can double-cross me. I have someone watching over your friend in the hospital. They have orders to kill her if they don't hear from me at a certain time every day."

Hawk was watching Ilse. "I guess I don't have much choice then, do I?"

"Not really, Mister Hawk. Come."

"Where are we going?" Hawk asked, confused.

"We are leaving. There is work to be done."

"You seem to forget I already work for someone else."

"Not anymore."

———

"WHERE IS HE?" Thurston demanded.

"He is gone," the officer in charge replied disinterestedly.

"What do you mean, he's gone?"

"People came and he left with them."

"What people?" Anja inquired.

"I do not know."

"Surely, they must have signed in?"

"I never see them before."

Thurston said, "Can't you at least have a look?"

Anja reached out and touched her arm. "Let's go. He's obviously not here. We'll find him."

Once outside the jail, Anja turned to Thurston. "Something isn't right. Jake wouldn't just go without telling us. There must be a reason."

"Then you have to find out. I need to go back to Herefordshire."

"Don't worry, I'll find him," Anja reassured her boss.

"I hope so. Before something happens."

———

"I HAVE SOMETHING," Karl said, as he brought his laptop in and set it in front of Anja. "Jake left with three people. I'm yet to identify them, but I don't think it will be a problem."

He pressed play and the video rolled, showing the four people leaving the jail. Anja watched in silence before saying, "I have a feeling I should know the woman. Her face seems familiar somehow."

"I agree. I'll have something for you as soon as I get it."

"What do you want me to do?" Gray asked. He had left the hospital as soon as the Interpol men had arrived. Anja had organized that.

"Go and see Jake's friend at the nightclub. Maybe it might give us a lead."

"Yes, boss."

Gray left the room, heading for his vehicle to brave the traffic, and thirty minutes later he reached the club. There was no one on the door so he went inside. "We're closed," a woman called out from behind the bar.

"I can appreciate that. I'm looking for Dejan."

The woman stared at him, alarm flickering across her face. "He's not here."

Gray could tell she was lying. He walked up to the bar, took out his Glock, and placed it on the wood top. "I just want to talk to him about last night."

She stared at the gun. "I already told you, he's not here."

"You're lying."

"No, I'm not."

"Yes, you are."

"It's all right," a voice said. "Go and tidy up out back, Kristina."

Gray took the gun from the bar and tucked it inside his pants while the girl left. He turned and looked at Kovac. "You're Dejan?"

"I am. Who are you to come here and threaten my staff?"

"I'm looking for Hawk," Gray said, ignoring the question.

"He's not here. The last I heard the police had him."

"What did he ask you?"

"Nothing, we talked about old times."

"You're lying, Dejan."

"Am I?"

Gray nodded. "What did he want to know?"

"I already told you. We—"

The sentence was cut off as Gray took a step forward, reached out, grabbed the club owner by the hair, and slammed his head down face first onto the polished countertop.

The thud was brutal and drew blood immediately as well as a large man with a gun who appeared at a rear door. The newcomer was too slow, for Gray already had his out and pointed at the back of the stunned Kovac's head. "Back off, mate, or I'll give your boss a one-way trip to hell."

"What—what are you doing?" Kovac pleaded.

"I'm just after answers to questions."

"He asked me who was specializing in black girls. I told him nothing."

Gray pressed the barrel of his Glock down hard on the back of the club owner's head. "You sure about that?"

"Yes, yes. I told him nothing."

Gray let him go and Kovac stood up, dabbing at his bleeding nose. "You are fucking crazy. Just like Jake."

"That remains to be seen," Gray said and started to

walk towards the door. Then he stopped and turned. "Who is trading in black girls in Belgrade?"

"Fuck off."

———

"HE'S NOT TALKING," Gray said. "The only answer I got was that he told Jake nothing."

Anja nodded. "Well, we had a development while you were gone. Our mystery woman has a name. Desarae Peeters. She's Belgian."

Anja slid a picture across the table for Gray to look at. "She's an attractive lass."

"She's dangerous. She's like a black widow spider and viper all mixed into one."

"I can understand that. Who is she when she's at home?"

"Desarae is, as I said, Belgian. She flies mostly under the radar but back when I was working with German intelligence she was more or less running her father's business."

"What was that?" Gray asked.

"He was an arms dealer for certain countries in Africa. Mostly the DRC and Sierra Leone. Although he used to supply weapons to certain factions in South Africa and terrorist organizations in Nigeria as well."

"What happened?" Gray asked Anja. "You said 'was'."

"He was killed in an operation to intercept an arms shipment in Nigeria."

"French? British?"

"German. I was in command."

"Shit a brick," Gray hissed.

"Exactly. If she's picked out Jake, it's for a specific reason. My name being at the top of the list."

The door opened and Karl appeared. "I managed to find some more information about our friend."

"Go on."

"She has the penthouse suite booked at the Belgrade Gardens. Funnily enough, she owns it."

"The penthouse?" Gray asked.

"No, the hotel."

Anja said, "If she went after Jake, it means she knew he was here. It also means she knows the rest of us are here."

"I have more," Karl interrupted.

They both looked at him expectantly. "I was searching through security feed from the hotel which I managed to procure—"

"That's a big word, Karl," Gray said.

"It is for the uneducated."

The Brit chuckled. "Carry on, Squire."

Karl opened the laptop he carried and placed it down so they could see the screen. "This is some of the feed I got."

Karl froze it. Two people in the foyer, talking. "That's our lady there and look who she's talking to."

Anja's eyes narrowed. "Rolf Balzer."

"Yes. Now the question is, what was their relationship?"

"It has to be Medusa."

"But why not kill Jake?" Gray asked.

"They tried," Karl said hurriedly. "At the jail."

Anja and the Brit turned their heads to look at Karl.

"Right before she came to see him, two men were put into a yard with Jake. He killed them both."

Gray nodded. "It was a test. She wants to use him which explains why she never killed him when she had the chance."

"I'll buy that," Anja agreed. "But what is it they want him for?"

"Whatever it is, it can't be good."

"Flash place you have here," Hawk said as he looked around the exquisite penthouse suite. He opened the bedroom door and saw a double king bed, messed up from sleeping. "Big bed, too."

"If you don't mind, Mister Hawk, I would rather we discussed business than whatever it is that you're trying to do. Like looking for a way out, maybe?"

"Habit," Hawk replied. "Always look for the nearest point of exfil just in case."

Desarae's two bodyguards retreated to different corners of the room, putting plenty of distance between them so Hawk, should he try to overcome them, wouldn't be able to.

The woman poured two glasses of vodka, offering the Talon operative one. He sipped it and pulled a face. Vodka just wasn't his thing. He put it down on a counter and said, "All right, you want to talk business, then talk."

"The place you will infiltrate is run by a woman named Natalija Novak."

"I know her name."

"Yes, but I can get you in."

"All right, what then?"

"You will pose as one of her bodyguards," Desarae told him. "From there you will have access to everything. I want bank account numbers to start with. That is the main thing."

"What about Hermann?"

"What about him?"

"I want him."

Novak's face hardened, her dark eyes smoldering. "You will do as I say."

Hawk set his jaw firm. "I want Hermann."

"I think you are getting confused as to who is actually in charge here, Jacob," the woman said sternly.

"You should do that more often."

"What?" She was confused.

"Get angry, it's kind of hot." A broad grin split his lips. "Actually, it's really hot."

"Are you trying to fuck me, Jacob?"

"Maybe. I have a thing for bad girls."

She smiled at him. "Trust me, the last thing you want to do is sleep with me."

Hawk moved forward. He stopped when they were almost touching. He stared into her eyes, smiling. "Maybe I'm willing to risk it."

She reached out and touched his chest. "Maybe I am, too."

He moved in closer, leaning forward about to kiss her on the lips when she ducked away. "There is a room for you down the hall. I will see you tomorrow."

Hawk nodded. "I guess you will."

———

THE ROOM WAS BIG, not as big as the one Desarae was in, but still it was a good size. He painstakingly walked around the room searching for any bugs that might be hidden there. He found none. Not even a camera. "Trusting lot this bunch."

However, they weren't trusting enough not to leave a guard out in the hallway. The Talon operative slid back the sliding glass door opening onto the balcony. He looked over the railing. Twenty floors straight down.

A grim expression came to Hawk's face. He turned, closed the sliding door and then went back to the railing. With a deep sigh, he said, "I don't know why I do this shit."

Then he climbed over the railing and began his descent, floor by floor.

Twenty minutes later, Hawk was on the ground. Using the shadows to his advantage, he made his way out onto the street and turned left. He didn't have a cell, so he'd have to find a place to get one.

It wasn't long until he found a late-night store which sold prepaid ones. Pulling his wallet from his pocket, he placed the box on the counter and paid for it. Then, minutes later, it was ready to go.

"Hello?"

"It's me, I don't have much time, just listen."

"Where are you, Jake?" Anja asked.

"That doesn't matter, boss. Listen, you have to have Gray keep an eye on Ilse. She's in danger."

"I can do that, but tell me what's going on?"

"I was taken from the jail by a woman named Desarae Peeters. She thinks I'm working for her. I guess in a way I am."

"What do you mean?"

Hawk started walking back towards the hotel. "She wants me to kill Ilya Noskov."

"How?"

"By luring him out of hiding," Hawk replied.

"Again, how?"

"By continuing with the mission we started."

"What is her end game, Jake?" Anja asked.

"Get this, the silly cow wants to break it all up. Make Medusa nonexistent and keep the best bits for herself."

"Tell me where you are, and we'll come and get you."

"No, I'm going to see this through."

"Jake, it's a crazy idea."

"Just make sure that Ilse is looked after. And be ready. If Noskov does come out of hiding the shit will really hit the fan. I have to go."

"Damn it, Jake, be careful."

"You know me."

"Yes, I do."

"I'll reach out when I can."

The call disconnected and Hawk headed back to the hotel.

CHAPTER TEN

Belgrade, Serbia

THE FOLLOWING morning a knock on the door was followed by a room attendant entering with a breakfast cart. Close behind him was the guard who'd been stationed outside the door.

"Breakfast, sir," the attendant said.

"Not really that hungry," Hawk said.

"I think you'll like this one, sir. The chef spent a lot of time on it. Knife and fork in under the top shelf. Also there is something to put on as well."

Hawk's face remained passive. Was the attendant trying to tell him something? The Talon operative nodded. "All right, leave it there."

The attendant left the room followed by the guard. Hawk immediately moved towards the trolley and lifted the cloth to reveal a package beneath. He picked it up and turned it over before opening it. What he found was what appeared to be a pair of longjohns, an old one-piece suit of underwear. But it wasn't anything like that. This was state of the art stuff. Something the Global Corporation had been working on for a while; had spent millions developing. The fabric was Synoprathetic and it had the capability of stopping most caliber rounds fired from assault rifle or handgun. Its weakness was that it wouldn't completely stop the high velocity rounds which larger caliber sniper rifles fired. The fabric itself was light and felt like wearing a second skin. That was where it came into its own. The wearer could run, roll, fight hand to hand without the restrictions of wearing body armor. Sure, the operator had to wear the webbing with ammo pouches and such, but it was still better.

It came with a note. WEAR IT. A.

Hawk undressed and put the suit on. It fitted well and was completely hidden beneath his street clothes. Then he checked his breakfast. Bacon and eggs. "Just what the doctor ordered," he said and hooked in.

He was almost finished when Desarae entered his room. There was no warning, just the door opening and she was there with two of her bodyguards. "We are leaving."

Hawk stared at her. She was wearing dark pants and a loose-fitting shirt. Over the top of it was a black jacket and he could see the bulge underneath the left side which indicated a hidden weapon. "Where are we going?"

"To see Natalija."

"I'm almost finished my breakfast."

"You are finished now."

"Bossy, aren't you?"

"Do not test me, Jacob. Remember, I still hold the better hand."

Hawk nodded, putting his knife and fork down. "I need a weapon."

The second of the two bodyguards had been carrying a small case. He passed it to Hawk. The Talon man opened it and found a Glock inside along with ammunition and spare magazines.

Beside them was a burner cell. When he picked it up,

Desarae said, "It has one number in it. Mine. It also has a tracking chip as well. That way I can keep an eye on you. I expect daily reports each night. Once you have accessed the account numbers you will be able to use the phone as an uplink, and my technician will do the rest."

"You do realize that it might take a few days to get to that point, don't you?" Hawk asked her.

"I'm a patient woman, Jacob. Just don't test me."

He smiled at her. "I wouldn't dream of it."

"And remember, the life of your friend depends on it."

"You know, you're going about it the wrong way," Hawk put to her.

"What do you mean?" Desarae's curiosity was piqued.

"Just let me loose and I'll dismantle it. No restraints. Hermann will come to see what's happening and when he does, we take him out, too."

Hawk could see the woman was indeed interested in what he was saying. "What about Noskov?"

"I'll arrange for him to find out. When he does, I'm sure he will put in an appearance. Then I'll make good on our arrangement."

"If I decide to do this, why would I need you? I have enough of my own men to do it."

"You may have enough men, but none of your men are like me, Desarae. Not one."

She stared at him, her mind ticking over. Then she shook her head. "No. Why would I dismantle it when I can take it over?"

"Because you don't have any choice, Desarae. If you want my help, we do it my way."

"Once again you forget that I have a jack in the hole."

"It's called an ace, love. And so do I." He took out the phone he'd bought the night before. "I also have someone watching. And I guarantee, they are much better than your person."

There was a deep-seated anger in Desarae's eyes. She

disliked not having the upper hand. "When this is over, I will kill you, Jacob."

"Get in line, love. It's a bloody long one."

Desarae emitted a sound from her throat which reminded Hawk somewhat of a tomcat about to fight another encroaching upon its territory.

"Tell me what you know about the operation."

"They bring the blacks in on trucks. Hidden amongst the cargo in containers. After arriving at the yard, they are distributed from there. The suitable ones go to Amsel Haus. The rest are dispersed elsewhere."

Hawk said. "What else? Does she have a head of security?"

"Yes. His name is Kaspar Haas."

"Does he live at the house?"

"No. He has a place not far away. I'm not sure where it is."

"Find out."

Desarae stared hard at him.

"What are you going to do?"

"I'm going to kill him. Oh, I'll need wheels."

Desarae nodded to one of her bodyguards. The man went to his jacket pocket and retrieved a key fob. "Porsche Cayenne, nice. Where is it?"

"Parking garage. I want it back in one piece."

"I will do my best but I make no guarantees," Hawk replied, remembering his relationship with vehicles of late wasn't that great. "Don't wait up, dear. Text me the address."

"Where are you going?"

"To have a look at Amsel Haus." He'd almost reached the door before he stopped, turned, and tossed the cell she'd given him onto the floor. "I won't be needing that either."

A couple of heartbeats later he was gone.

Desarae stared after him. "Fucking asshole."

ANJA'S CELL buzzed and she hurriedly answered it. "Jake?"

"Yeah, it's me."

"What's going on?"

"I'm working on something to try and get Hermann to Belgrade where we can take him out."

"What happens after that?"

"Hopefully Noskov will materialize like a magician, and we can get a crack at him, too."

"What if we could almost guarantee that he would come?"

"I'm listening."

"I will talk to Leonid Federov. Maybe he can tell us how to get a message to Noskov."

"You mean tip him off?" Hawk asked.

"Something like that. Tell him that Desarae has turned on him. Maybe that will be enough for him to come out and make an example of her himself."

"It might work," agreed Hawk. "Or he'll send a murder team and take half of Belgrade off the map to get to her."

"There is that. Did you get my present?"

"I did, thank you. How is Ilse?"

"Better. And before you ask, Gray is watching her. It only took him five minutes to make Desarae's watchers."

"Watchers?"

"Yes, there are two."

"Tell him to be careful. She knows we have a man there."

"I'll pass it on."

"I have to go. Remember this number." He rattled it off. "Did you get it?"

"Yes."

"You can reach me on that. I'll call when I have something."

"Jake..."

"Don't say it."

Hawk stopped. He was in the hotel parking garage looking for the Porsche when the three black Range Rover SUVs came in. "Hold on, boss."

"What's up, Jake?"

"I'm not sure, stay on the line."

He kept the cell in his left hand while reaching around his back to grab the Glock. He took it from his waistband and held it down alongside his leg. The three SUVs came to a halt beside each other, and eight men climbed out and moved to the rear of them.

Hawk watched as they placed duffel bags on the ground and unzipped them. Before long they were passing weapons and tactical gear around. Each weapon looked to be suppressed AK-12s.

The Talon operative put the cell up to speak again but another loud sound drew his attention. A delivery van almost opposite to where the SUVs had parked suddenly disgorged another eight shooters. Every one of them was ready to go.

"Shit," he hissed and retreated behind a concrete pillar. He put the cell up to his ear. "Boss, you still with me?"

"What's going on, Jake?"

"I think Noskov already knows what Desarae is up to."

He disconnected the call.

————

HAWK FIGURED that the kill squad—for without doubt, that is what it was—could have worked their operation one of two ways. They could do it surgically, with a minimum amount of carnage, or they could go in all guns blazing and shoot everything that moved making a statement. Somehow, he had the feeling that it wasn't going to be the first option which meant a lot of innocent people were about to become collateral damage.

It was about then he wished he had kept the cell with Desarae's number in it. Not that he cared what happened to her, but it might have saved lives somehow. But here he was, one gun against sixteen. "Shit fucking odds at the best of times," he muttered.

Hawk fumbled with his cell until he was able to find the number for the hotel on Google. A couple of rings later and a woman's voice answered. "Welcome to—"

"Listen closely," Hawk whispered harshly, cutting her off. "You need to shut the hotel down and inform your security that there are armed gunmen in the parking garage."

"I beg your pardon, sir?"

"There are armed men in your parking garage, love. Get your security to lock down the fucking hotel."

"I'm sorry, sir, but there is no need for such language."

Fuck a duck! "I'm sorry, but—"

The sound of footsteps caused Hawk to stop.

"Sir?"

The shooters started to make their way past where he stood, and Hawk held his breath. Inside his chest his heart beat thunderously as though he was going into combat for the first time.

The footsteps started to fade away and Hawk said into the cell, "Get out of the hotel."

"I'm sorry, sir, but—"

Hawk never heard the rest because he was more concerned with the pressure on his spine. He slowly raised his hands and said, "Bugger it."

"Turn around."

The Talon operative turned slowly and came face to

face with a man about his own height but wearing tactical gear, a radio headset, and carrying an AK-12. But that wasn't what was trained on him at the minute. It was an MP-443 Grach handgun.

"Who are you?" the man asked in an accented voice.

"Would you believe tourist?"

"Ha, you are funny," the man snorted and shot Hawk point blank in the chest.

The shooter turned and walked away, leaving Hawk on the cold hard concrete, gasping for breath. The would-be killer didn't even bother to check that Hawk was out of the fight. If he had, he would have seen a lack of one very telltale sign. Blood. There wasn't any.

"Frigging gobshite bastard," the Talon operative moaned. It felt as if he'd been kicked in the chest by a horse. However, he'd been shot before in body armor, and it had hurt worse. Little did he know at the time, but the special weave of the synthetic fabric of the body suit cushioned some of the shock from the blow when it was hit by a bullet.

Hawk had dropped his gun and his right hand reached out and grabbed it. He rolled over, pain burning his body, raised the weapon he held, and squeezed the trigger.

Over the low foresight of the Glock he saw the bullet impact the back of the departing man's skull. Lurching forward, the man fell face down on the hard concrete.

Hawk climbed to his feet and winced. He looked down and saw the hole in his shirt but no blood. "Would have hurt less if the bastard had shot me proper," he moaned.

The Talon operative walked over and bent down, picking up the AK-12 and the webbing with extra magazines. He slipped into it and checked the AK to make sure it would fire when he needed it.

Then he turned towards the elevators and growled, "Right, now I'm pissed."

INSTEAD OF GOING STRAIGHT for the penthouse floor, Hawk went to the lobby. He needed to get the elevators shut down so he could funnel the shooters into one of the stairwells.

As he climbed off the elevator he saw the first dead security guard outside the doors, laying in a pool of blood.

Hawk brought up the AK and started to sweep the area before him. He could hear the shouts of alarm and then the sound of suppressed gunfire somewhere near the counter. Their idea was obviously to secure the lobby and seal off the exit. The question was how many of them were on the floor?

This was answered soon enough when he emerged from behind a pillar and could see the open plan area before him.

Four. One at the desk, another at the entrance, and a third checking on a downed security guard. The fourth was starting to round up prisoners and seat them on a large mat in the center of the room.

Secure the hostages.

The AK came up and the Talon operative peered through the Steiner MRS red dot sight on top of the assault weapon. As soon as the dot itself settled on the fourth man's head, he squeezed the trigger.

The man's head snapped back, and a small puff of red mist sprayed into the air, signaling that the shot had gone true. Hawk shifted his aim to the man beyond them at the entrance. This time he wasn't as fussy and fired three shots at him.

The shooter dropped to the floor, two of the three bullets doing irreparable damage. The shooter's weapon clattered to the hard floor making the sound echo.

By this time the other two shooters began responding to what was happening.

The one near the counter opened fire and Hawk was forced to take cover behind the pillar to his right. Bullets hammered into it, ricocheting, gouging out large chips.

"Asshole bastard," Hawk growled before leaning back out and opening fire.

The shooting stopped as the dying man collapsed, and the Talon operative heard the remaining man shouting into his radio.

Hawk searched for him, but he had disappeared behind cover somewhere across the lobby. The Talon operative came out into the open and pressed forward searching for the final target.

The group of prisoners on the mat were becoming anxious about their futures, their fear heightened. "Stay down!" Hawk barked at them. "Don't move."

But the fear was overwhelming for most and eventually became too much. It only took one person to lunge to their feet and start running before the rest followed.

"No! Stop!"

They were beyond reason, and nothing was going to stop them from escaping out the door to freedom. So, they ran—

Just as the man came up from where he was hiding behind a leather sofa and opened fire.

The aiming was indiscriminate even though the long burst was meant for Hawk. People fell like autumn leaves, spasming under the impact of the hailstorm.

"Get down! Get down!" Hawk shouted repeatedly until his throat burned. Words which fell on deaf ears and failed to pierce uncomprehending minds.

The Talon operator brought up the AK, seeking to make a clear shot but the fog of people blocked everything. He lowered it, brought it up, then lowered it once more. The next time he raised the assault weapon the mass of fleeing people seemed to part revealing the shooter beyond. "Got you."

Hawk squeezed the trigger and the weapon kicked back into his shoulder. The bullet struck the shooter in the head, and he fell back behind the sofa.

The Talon operative looked around at the carnage: wounded and dead lying on the cold hard floor in pools of blood. A woman dressed in a hotel uniform was running past him and he grabbed her by her blouse. Her momentum carried her around and she almost crashed into him with the pressure of her snagged uniform. She jerked to a stop and squealed in panic.

"Hey, I'm on your side. Listen to me."

She stared at him goggle eyed.

"You need to call the police and then call for ambulances. A lot of them. Okay?" He held her by both upper arms, looking her in the eyes, trying to break through the fearful miasma emanating from her.

She glanced at the door, looking like a wild animal fleeing from a hunter.

Hawk tried again, giving her a small shake to snap her out of it. "Hey! Do you understand what I'm saying? These people need you to do this."

"Okay."

"Where do I shut down the elevators?"

"What?"

She wasn't with it. He couldn't blame her, not after what she'd just witnessed. "The elevators. I need to shut them down. Where do I do that?"

"The basement. The switchboard."

Hawk shook his head. Go down, do it, then take the stairs back up. Waste of time. "Stuff it. Just make the calls."

"Okay."

"And tell them there is one friendly in the building. They can identify me by—" He looked around then saw the red and blue scarf around her throat. Hawk reached out and took it, eliciting a gasp from the woman, before wrapping it around his face, which had him resembling an outlaw from a western movie. "Tell them about the scarf. I don't want them killing me by mistake. Understood?"

"Okay." She nodded hesitantly.

"Shit," Hawk muttered and started running towards the elevator bank.

He got off on nineteen before heading to the stairwell. Hawk looked up and saw nothing, it seemed to be clear. Keeping the AK-12 up at his shoulder, the Talon operative started climbing.

Hawk eased through the door leading onto the floor and saw his first body. Surprisingly it wasn't one of Desarae's people. It was an attacker. He'd been shot through the face and left where he'd fallen. A few feet past him lay the body of his killer.

Hawk moved on finding more bodies, both attackers and defenders. The Brit realized that Desarae had more bodyguards than he figured. Well-armed, too. Upon reaching the suite, he found the door open.

He discovered more bodies inside but found no sign of the Medusa operators. Obviously, their team had hit with precision, gotten the job done, departing as quickly as they had come via the elevators.

Hawk found Desarae on the floor of the master suite. She'd been shot twice in the chest. It was strange but Hawk thought she looked even more attractive in death.

The Talon operator sighed. "Well, you died the same way that you lived, but we'll see if we can finish what you set out to do."

Hawk reached into his pocket and took out the cell he'd bought. "Yeah, I need a pickup."

CHAPTER ELEVEN

Belgrade, Serbia

THE THREE OF them sat around the table discussing the turn of events. Hawk fingered a glass of scotch as Karl ran down a list of what he had discovered and what they knew.

"Somehow Noskov knew what Desarae had planned which would indicate that he had someone on the inside."

"Pretty self-explanatory," Hawk said with a patronizing tone.

Anja glared at him.

Karl continued, "From what I could find from the few pictures that Jake took of the dead, as per usual, they were already dead by some years."

"Again—"

"Jacob!" Anja snapped.

It was his turn to return the glare, but she remained unperturbed. "What?" he asked.

"Continue, Karl," she said, ignoring the Brit.

"The vehicles they used were obviously stolen and when they were found by authorities, I was able to find out that they had been painted over before being used. No discernable fingerprints or anything like that."

"Why not just burn them?" Hawk asked.

"They obviously thought they didn't need to. Which was pure arrogance on their part."

"Perhaps we need to consider the possibility that they have the police in their pockets and *knew* they didn't have to," Anja said.

"Correct. That was how Desarae was able to get Jake out of his predicament."

"Have you been able to figure out where they went?" Hawk asked.

Karl shook his head. "No. My guess is that they're out of the country by now. In, do the job, and extract once the mission's complete."

"At least Ilse will be safer now," Hawk said. "Do we take Gray off her?"

"Not yet," Anja replied. "Let's see where this takes us."

"So, we continue as planned?" Hawk asked.

"Yes. But while we're doing that, I'll see if I can find out anything on Noskov. I've had enough of fucking around. It's time to end it."

The Brit gave a nod. "Karl, I need to know all about Kaspar Haas and where he is residing."

"I can do that. Is there a reason?"

"Yes, so I can kill him."

"As good as any," he said with a shrug.

"Explain, Jake," Anja said.

"I'm going to take out their head of security," Hawk explained. "Then while they're dealing with that, I'm getting inside and stealing the account numbers to every red cent they have."

"Can't Karl do that?"

The tech shook his head. "No—well, yes, but only if you have a month to spare."

"All right, let's go to work. In the meantime, I have a flight to catch and an old friend to speak with."

———

Somewhere in Europe

Leonid Federov took one look at the woman entering the small room and smiled. "We meet in person; this must be important."

The guard who had led her through walked over to a corner and stood still as Anja sat down opposite the high-security prisoner. She stared at Federov before saying, "You have one chance to get this right, Leonid. You start screwing me and I'll have Andre waterboard your ass until fish swim out of your fucking mouth."

"As much as screwing you sounds inviting, the swimming lessons I can do without. What is the issue I can help you with today?" His tone was amiable.

"I need to know where I can find Ilya Noskov."

The Russian snorted scornfully. "And I need to pull a million dollars out of my ass, but it isn't going to happen."

Anja leaned forward. "Then you had better consider how to make it possible because I plan on leaving here with an answer."

"I don't know what to say."

"Think of something."

"How? You have given me nothing."

"Two days ago, he sent a team to kill Desarae Peeters in Belgrade," Anja informed him.

"I bet that was messy," Federov replied.

"A total disaster. But they got the job done."

"Why did he kill her?"

"She was trying to lure him out to kill him."

"Greed." Federov shook his head.

"Not from what I can gather. She was going to keep

the good bits for herself, yes, but thought that it was all too much for one person."

"Do you know who was leading the team?"

"No."

"You know he could be anywhere?"

Anja nodded. "I am well aware of that. What I want to know is where he's *most likely* to be."

Federov looked thoughtful for a moment, steepling his fingers and placing them under his chin. "It would have to be somewhere out of the way, somewhere that no one would suspect him to be."

"Where would Medvedev have gone?"

"Tagomago Island."

"Ibiza?"

"Yes."

"I thought that was just for rent?"

"No, Medvedev bought it a couple of years ago under the umbrella of a tourist company. If I had to guess, he would be there."

"I don't need guesses, I need assurances."

"Alas, there are no assurances but it is the best I can do. If he is anywhere, that will be it. It's secure. You would have to send an army to get him out."

Anja stared hard at him. "That is something I don't need to worry about. I already have an army."

Belgrade, Serbia

At five terrace houses along the street north of their target, the van rolled to a stop. Gray killed the headlights and turned the motor off. "Target building in sight," he said into his comms to let Karl know they had arrived.

"Roger that, Bravo Two. You're on site. The screen at my end looks clear."

"Copy, Alpha." There was a pause and Gray said, "Comms check, Jake."

"All clear, Marcus. Shall we earn a quid?"

"Let's do it."

Hawk took out his Glock 19 and checked it before alighting from the van. His feet touched the wet pavement and made a gritty sound which seemed louder than it was, due to his heightened senses.

He closed the door and started along the sidewalk towards the target building which Haas was supposedly in.

"Jake, I've got a vehicle turning into the street ahead of you," Karl warned him.

Hawk turned away as the headlights illuminated him so the driver wouldn't see his face. Once it had passed, he started walking again.

"All clear, Jake."

The streetlamps were well spaced being a residential neighborhood, which went in their favor. The less lighting the better.

Halfway there, and in a semi-blackspot, Hawk crossed the street and stepped up onto the opposite sidewalk.

As he approached the target building, he said, "How are we looking, Alpha?"

"All clear, Bravo One."

Making a sharp right turn Hawk hurried up the steps to the front door. Holding a pen light in his mouth to illuminate the lock, he picked it quickly and opened the door.

"Eight, four, three, seven, seven, nine, three, nine," Karl said deliberately.

Once inside the door, Hawk immediately turned to his right where he punched the numbers into the pad to disable the night alarm.

It quietly beeped twice and then the small light on the panel changed to green. "Alarm disengaged," he whispered.

"Copy."

Beneath his clothes, Hawk could feel the comfort of the Synoprathetic suit. His body was bruised where he'd been shot, but the fabric had stopped the bullet for which he was grateful. He just hoped he didn't get shot too often.

"The main bedroom should be up the stairs and along the hallway directly in front of the landing," Karl informed him.

"Copy."

Hawk climbed the stairs slowly, making sure of his footing as he went. When he reached the second to last from the top it seemed to scream under his weight.

Shit!

When nothing happened, he took another step and reached the landing.

After waiting several heartbeats, he started down the hall, past the room on his left and right, closing in on the door in front of him.

Hawk stopped and reached out to turn the knob.

Suddenly the door exploded outward toward him. Not on its hinges like a normal swinging door, but as though a great blast had blown it from within like in the movies. Except this time, what followed wasn't an orange fireball, but a 260-pound monster complete with black beard.

"Fuck a duck!" Hawk cried out in shock, withdrawing his hand as he fell back, the door and behemoth landing on top of him, crushing the air from his lungs, sending the Glock spilling from his grasp.

Stunned, he lay there and moaned while in his ear he could hear Gray saying, "Jake, are you all right? Jake, answer me. Damn it, Jake—"

The door on top of Hawk wobbled as Haas rolled off it, the sudden reduction in weight a sweet relief. Then the giant of a man picked it up and tossed it aside.

Dappled light filtering in from outside through a

hallway window illuminated the scene sufficiently for Hawk to get a glimpse of the hulking figure before him.

Intelligence failure, the Talon operative thought. *So much for him being six feet.*

Haas was closer to six five, making him a touch taller than Hawk. Which explained the force he was able to exert upon the door. Haas reached down and grabbed Hawk by the collar of his shirt, dragging him to his feet.

Still muddled from the hard hit, Hawk failed to deflect the savage blow coming his way as it crashed against his jaw.

The Talon operative fell back against the wall, jarring his spine. Hawk gritted his teeth against the pain while his vision clouded.

"Talk to me, Jake," Gray said in his ear.

Haas closed in and ripped a blow to Hawk's body. He grunted and felt his legs buckle instinctively as he tried to protect himself.

Haas hit Hawk again; this time the Brit expected it and turned slightly, cushioning the blow. With his head starting to clear, Hawk lashed out, a fist finding the mark. Haas shook his head from the blow to the jaw and renewed his assault with a flurry of punches. Hawk covered up as they rained down.

Suddenly Hawk thrust his arms forward, shoving Haas backward. The resulting impact shook the hallway. Hawk closed in and started to mete out his own punishment.

Bone-jarring blows to the body and jaw rocked Haas on his heels, but somehow, he managed to push Hawk back and the Talon operative stumbled before falling to the floor.

Pain shot through his side as Haas kicked him in the ribs. The big man's foot drew back to deliver another brutal blow but Hawk rolled to his left, crashing into the wall.

Now instead of the side, the toe of the man's foot drove into Hawk's back causing more pain to rip through his body.

Almost instantly, Hawk became aware of the hard object he was laying on. He reached down and his right hand grasped the butt of the Glock he had lost.

Hawk brought the weapon around and up, firing twice. Both rounds punched into Haas's chest and made him stagger. To make sure, Hawk fired twice more and the man before him fell backwards with a crash.

"Jake, are you alright? Speak to me, pal."

Hawk groaned. "Come and pick me up, Marcus. Mission complete."

———

"TAGOMAGO ISLAND?" Hawk asked for confirmation.

Anja nodded. "Yes."

"So, what's the plan?"

"We confirm his presence and then go in after him."

"Until then?"

"We continue what we started here."

Hawk nodded. "The next phase being, getting into Amsel Haus and stealing the account numbers."

"Yes."

"Any notion on how we do that?" Hawk asked.

"It was your idea."

"You know," Gray started, "I watched an American movie a long time back where they posed as pest exterminators to get inside this cartel bloke's house. We could try something like that."

"Bad Boys," Hawk said.

"Yeah, that's it. Those guys were batshit crazy."

"No, the movie. Bad Boys Two."

"Okay. It was that long ago I have no idea."

"Won't work. Who's going to believe two Tommies turning up to exterminate whatever the fuck they have?"

"It might work if it was one Tommy and a German," Anja said.

"You coming with?" Hawk asked.

She nodded. "Keep my hand in."

"Fine, but we need a plan because if this goes sideways, we're going to be in trouble."

Anja looked at Karl. "Can you get us what we need?"

He nodded. "Give me a day and I'll have it for you."

"Another thing. When we get the account numbers, I want some of the money put into our own accounts."

"We already have at least two-hundred million," Karl pointed out.

"I want more. It takes money to keep an operation like ours running."

"What happens when the headshed finds out?" Hawk asked.

"Thurston already knows. She was the one who authorized it."

Hawk nodded. "In that case, the beers are on you."

"Check the refrigerator."

He grinned.

"I almost forgot, how did the Synoprathetic suit go?"

Hawk rubbed his chest. "Is there any way you can put some cushioning in it?"

"Get shot, did we?" Anja raised a questioning eyebrow.

"Maybe."

"Take your shirt off and let me look at it," Anja said.

Hawk glanced at the others who were grinning at him.

"I'm sure Marcus and Karl have other things they can do."

"Yes, boss," Gray said, climbing to his feet. "Come on, Karl, show me that thing of yours."

Karl's grin got wider. "Right away. Good luck, Jake."

"Shut it or I'll mess up your desk."

They left the room and Anja stared at Hawk.

"What?"

"Take your shirt off."

He mumbled under his breath and did as he was told. Once it was removed, he turned to face her. Anja winced. Through the thick mat of hair covering his torso she could see the large, purplish bruise. She reached out and tenderly touched around it. "Does it hurt?"

"Not as much as it used to."

"I guess we can safely say the suits work."

He stiffened as she pressed in the wrong place. "I guess so."

Anja stared into his eyes. "It's a good thing you had it."

"Uh, huh."

"All right, put your shirt back on. I don't think anything is broken."

Hawk grinned at her, the discomfort gone. "And here I was starting to enjoy your tender ministrations."

She stabbed his bruise with her finger causing him to react to the shot of pain. "Holy shit, what did you do that for?"

"Just to remind you who your boss is."

"It was just a joke."

"I don't like jokes."

"I'll remember that."

"Please do."

"Do you mind if I go and see Ilse?"

Anja's expression softened. "No. I'm sure she would like to see you. But you should go now."

"Thanks, boss."

CHAPTER TWELVE

Belgrade, Serbia

HAWK HATED HOSPITALS. The sterile, overwhelming smell of disinfectant, bleach, bland food, and whatever else was mixed into it. Then there were the sounds: the alarms and cries of people in pain, not to mention the beeping of electronic machinery monitoring every heartbeat and more, or keeping patients alive.

Hawk stared at the heart monitor, its rhythmic peaks as it kept time with Ilse's heart. "Are you going to say hello?" she asked sleepily.

"I didn't want to wake you."

"I'm awake now."

"Then hello."

"I'm glad you came to see me, Jake."

"Couldn't stay away anymore. The boss made me come."

Ilse knew he was lying. "I'm sure she did. How are things?"

"Aw, you know, busy." He gave a small shrug.

"You saved my life, Jacob," she said in a soft voice.

He shrugged again. "I guess all that training the British government put into me has finally paid off."

Ilse reached for his hand but hers fell back to the bed. Instead, Hawk reached out and took it. "Hey, take it easy."

A tear formed at the corner of her eye and ran down her cheek, leaving a glistening trail behind it. "Can't you be serious for once?"

Hawk shook his head. "No. Serious reminds me of just how close we came to losing you. And I don't want to think about that."

"I'm fine, Jake. The doctor says I'll make a full recovery."

He ignored her statement. "We're working on a plan to get Noskov."

"Jake—"

He withdrew his hand.

"You need to look after yourself, Ilse," he said to her. "I'll come and visit when I can."

Her eyes blazed. "Damn you, Jacob Hawk."

He nodded. "I already am. Take care, Ilse."

As he walked through the door, he thought he heard her begin to sob.

————

"HOW WAS THE VISIT?" Anja asked Hawk.

"Fine."

"Is there something I need to know about, Jake?"

He turned to face her. "Like what?"

"Are you two involved?"

"No." It wasn't a lie.

"Are you sure?"

"I'm sure."

"Fine, we'll leave it at that. Now, come with me. Let's discuss our plan."

They found Gray and Karl watching television with

Karl trying to explain to the Brit what was happening in the show, but failing dismally. Anja said, "If you two are ready, we've got a mission to plan for."

"When you are, boss," Gray replied, looking up.

Anja looked at Karl. "Where are we with our rodent infestation?"

"It was relatively easy to accomplish. A few dollars to the right kid and job is done. We received the call an hour ago. Job to be carried out first thing tomorrow morning."

Anja nodded. "And the equipment?"

"Again, a few dollars in the right hand and we've got what we need."

"Good. Jake and I will need a layout for the place in question. So we can study it."

"I can do one better. I can link into the security system."

"Terrific."

"Do we know anything about security itself?" Hawk asked.

"Six guards."

"Is that it?" Hawk asked, raising his eyebrows.

"That's all you need when you have Belgrade police in your pocket."

"Point taken."

Karl pushed folders out to all of them. As each one opened their file, they were greeted by a photo of a tall, athletic blonde woman with average looks. Her hair was tied back in a ponytail. "That is Natalija Novak. She runs the operation. Don't let the fact that she is a woman fool you; she's a very dangerous individual."

"Most former military are," Hawk said. "Has there been much reaction since Haas went for a dirt nap?"

"She made a call to Germany. I can only surmise that it was to Hermann. But I think we can safely say it was since these unsavory gentlemen were snapped coming through Belgrade International four hours ago."

"Can we get a better look at the bloke up front?" Hawk asked.

The picture grew and cleared.

"Shit," Hawk growled. "Lester Boyle."

"Who is Lester Boyle?" Anja asked.

"Leads a small team of mercs," Hawk explained. "The others with him will be Harris Taylor, John Paul, and Chalky Morris."

"Do they know you by sight?" Anja asked.

Hawk nodded.

"What about you, Marcus?"

"No, boss."

"Then we change the plan. Marcus will come in with me and Jake will be backup in the van should we get into trouble."

"I guess we don't have a choice."

"Not really."

"I'll keep an eye on things," Karl said. "At the moment they're not on site but if it changes...well."

"All right, we'll leave Jake in for the moment. In the meantime, a new package arrived earlier."

Anja pointed at a box in the corner.

Gray got off his seat and walked over to retrieve it. He picked it up and placed it on the table where they were seated.

"Birthday presents?" Hawk asked.

Anja gave him a mirthless smile. "Nothing for you, Jacob. You've already got yours."

It was then he realized what they were. "Synoprathetic suits."

"Yes, we all get one. Every time we are operational, I am making it mandatory that we put them on."

"Might get a bit smelly," Karl pointed out.

"There will be more coming," Anja assured him. "But in the meantime, we have to make do with what we have."

"Don't worry, Karl," Hawk said to him. "There is only one thing to remember when you put one on."

"What is that?"

"It still hurts like hell when you get shot."

———

THE COVERALLS FITTED WELL and hid the bulletproof suits beneath them. The van stopped in the turnaround and Anja and Gray waited. "Can you confirm, Karl?"

"Confirmed, ma'am, Boyle and his crew are on site."

"All right. Jake, you stay in the van. You'll be logged into our comms if anything happens. You'll need to come in if it all goes wrong."

Hawk nodded. "Copy, boss."

Anja and Gray climbed from the van. Both were unarmed, for they knew what was coming. Two men appeared and started to check them for hidden weapons. "What is wrong with you?" Anja asked.

"Just be quiet."

Once they were finished, the one in charge said, "You can go in now."

"Do you mind if we get some of our equipment from the vehicle?"

"Hurry up."

Both men were armed with MP5s and waited impatiently for them to get what they needed. Once they had their kits, they were escorted inside.

It was like walking back in time to a time when grandiose was king. The lobby was massive; carpeted floor, wide staircase, dark timber paneling on the walls, numerous artworks and statuary, and a large chandelier.

Behind a hardwood counter stood a dark-skinned woman wearing a red ballgown which seemed a little out of place for that time of the day.

"Can I help you?" she asked with a heavy accent.

Anja answered her in German.

The woman frowned. "I'm sorry, I don't understand."

"We are here to set baits and traps for your rodent infestation," she said, switching to English. "We will need access to the kitchen and other rooms."

The young lady nodded. "Please wait here."

She reached for a phone and pressed a button. A few heartbeats later she spoke several words then hung up. "My mistress will be here soon."

Mistress.

Anja and Gray walked away from the counter and pretended to look at a painting on the wall. He said, "Boss, we're not going to be able to do this without going loud."

"Possibly. We'll have to wait and see. Jake, can you hear me?"

"Loud and clear, boss."

A door opened and two people appeared. One was Novak and the other was Boyle. He eyed Gray warily and asked, "Who are you?"

Gray said nothing.

"I'm talking to you."

"He does not speak," Anja said. "Something happened to him as a child."

"Really? How convenient."

"It is for me. It means I don't have to listen to him complain."

Anja stared at Novak. "We are here for the rodents."

"What do you need to do?"

"We need access to the kitchen, basement, and a few other rooms just to make sure."

"To do what, exactly?"

"Just to set some traps and baits. It is a test to see how bad it is."

Novak nodded. "Fine. Talk to no one and stay out of the bedrooms."

"Thank you."

"And make it quick. We're open for business in twenty minutes."

Anja spoke to Gray in German. "You start with the basement, and I'll do this floor before going upstairs."

"No," Novak said firmly.

Anja looked at her.

Novak continued, "There is no need to go upstairs."

In her ear the Talon commander heard Karl say, "It doesn't matter, the office you need is on that floor."

Anja nodded. "Fine, we'll stick to this floor and the basement."

Novak said, "Marlene will show you where to go."

Novak and Boyle left them then and retreated the way they'd come.

Marlene said, "I will show you through to the kitchen and then take the gentleman down to the basement."

"Thank you."

———

"KARL I NEED you to trip the alarm," Anja said.

"Boss?"

"I need to get into the office and there are people in there. You need to trip the alarm so I can have time to do what I need to do."

"I'll try, ma'am."

"Jake, I need you ready to come in here if it all goes sideways."

"Ready, boss."

"Gray?"

"Just say the word."

"When the alarm goes off, make your way upstairs."

"All right, Karl, do it."

Anja backed into a shallow alcove and waited. Within

moments the fire alarms throughout the building started to go off.

The door to the office opened and Novak and Boyle appeared, turned away from where she was hiding, and proceeded along the hallway.

"Ma'am, you'll have maybe three minutes before they are shut down."

"Just keep an eye out."

"Yes, ma'am."

Anja hurried to the door and found it locked. With a hiss of irritation, she reached for her lockpicks.

"Two and a half minutes, ma'am."

It took a further twenty seconds to pick the lock and by the time she was inside and had the door shut, Anja was down to two.

Inside the office was just as lavish as the rest of the building. Plush carpet, log fire, polished hard wood desk, more artwork, dark panels, and a floor to ceiling window which took in a view of the expansive grounds.

Anja looked around and hurried across to the desk. She tried the top drawer and it slid open. She flicked through it hurriedly before closing it and starting on the next. "Where would you put them, Karl?"

"You're asking me, ma'am?"

"Trying to cut down time."

"Safe, maybe?"

"Where though?" she asked scanning the walls. Then before he could answer she said, "Found it."

Anja walked towards a landscape painting which hung near the fireplace. From the front it looked as though it was set just right, but on closer inspection it sat proud from the wall just a fraction too far.

The Talon leader ran her hands along the edge of the frame until she found what she was looking for. With a click the picture swung outwards revealing an electronic safe behind it.

144

"One minute."

"I'm well aware of it, Karl."

"Then you need to work faster, ma'am."

Anja reached into her pocket and retrieved her cell. By tapping a few keys, she activated it and placed it near the keypad. The screen changed and began ticking numbers over with blurring speed.

She watched them fly by with growing impatience. "Marcus, report."

"I'm outside with everyone else, ma'am, while they work out what's happening." His voice was low. "I think they might be missing you. They keep looking at me."

"Can they see you talking?"

"No, boss."

"Copy. Jake, are you ready?"

"Just say the word, boss."

Even while she talked, Anja's eyes never left the screen.

Come on, come on.

Then the alarm stopped.

"Time to go, ma'am," Karl said.

"In a moment."

"Not in a moment. Now."

"I need to know what's in this safe."

"Anja!" His voice was curt.

She let out a frustrated sigh just as the cell beeped. "I have it."

"Boss—"

"I'm opening the safe."

"Jake, standby, this could all go south very fast."

"Boss, get out," Hawk said into his comms.

"I've got something."

"Marcus, move now."

"On it."

Then Karl said, "They're coming along the hallway. It's too late."

THE DOOR swung open and the two of them stopped and stared at Anja. Boyle reached for a concealed handgun, but Novak stopped him. "What are you doing in here?"

"I'm setting baits," Anja replied, holding up a small paper packet of rat poison. The rodents were supposed to chew through the paper to get to the rodenticide within. "You did say we could have access to this floor."

Novak's eyes darted towards the painting which concealed the safe. Everything looked to be in place. "How did you get in here?"

"It was open."

"No, it wasn't. I locked it."

"I'm sorry, no, you didn't."

Novak stared at her.

Gray appeared and Anja's gaze shifted. "Have you finished?"

He nodded.

"Good. I'm done here, too. Let's go." She looked at Novak. "Will there be anything else?"

There was uncertainty in Novak's eyes but she shook her head. "No. When will you be back?"

"The day after tomorrow."

She nodded. "I will see you then."

They went outside and climbed into the van. Anja said, "Let's get out of here before they realize what is happening."

She tossed the bag back to Hawk. "In there you'll find a book. Start giving the numbers to Karl. We'll see what comes of them."

"Yes, boss."

"TALK TO ME, KARL," Anja said as she walked into the room where he was set up.

Hawk and Gray followed her.

"Out of all the numbers, I've found one which works. It looks like they cycle through them. The others are like they're deactivated."

"How much?"

"Fifty million."

"Nothing to be sneezed at," Hawk commented, raising his eyebrows.

"I still have a couple of numbers to check but I'm not hopeful."

Hawk took the book and tossed it on the desk near where Karl was working. When it landed, something small emerged from it and skipped across the desk before stopping on the edge.

Karl frowned and picked it up, examined it, and then looked at the others. "I think we may have a problem."

"Damn it," Anja growled.

Suddenly a proximity warning sounded, and Karl flicked to a different tab on his computer. Two SUVs disgorged eight men, all heavily armed.

"We've got to go," Hawk snapped.

"Agreed. Jake, cover the entry. We need to salvage what we can and burn the rest."

"MI6 are going to love us," Gray said.

"Let's move, people."

The former para dug into a pack for an incendiary device which they would set off, while Hawk scooped up an AK-12 and headed for the stairwell. "I'll give you a couple of minutes, boss, before I follow you."

They were on the first floor of an abandoned apartment complex with the van out the rear of the building. The hallway ran back to a door which opened out onto a balcony that ran around the interior for the complex had been built around a courtyard. From the landing they would be able to get down and then out.

"Don't miss the bus, Jake," Gray said.

"Wouldn't be the first time," he called back and ran out into the hallway.

He reached the top of the stairs just as the kill squad was coming up. Hawk opened fire and took down the two point-men before recoiling as a hailstorm of bullets screamed up towards him.

Hawk watched as old plaster and concrete rained down into the shaft. He changed his position and fired again at the men coming up.

A sound drew his attention and he looked down to see a fragmentation grenade rolling near his feet.

Ballsy!

Diving back through the opening of the doorway as it exploded, Hawk felt the displacement of air as the blast washed over him. His ears rang and dust and debris covered him from head to toe. "Love a frigging duck," he growled as he rolled over onto his back.

Through the gloom a figure emerged, armed, weapon to their shoulder as they searched for a target. Hawk brought the AK-12 up and fired. The figure jerked and cried out in pain before falling back and disappearing into the dusty fog.

Hearing shouts from the stairwell, Hawk scrambled to his feet.

"Time to go, Jake," he muttered to himself and began a slow jog back along the hallway to the rear door.

Behind him a weapon opened up and bullets cracked past him. He dived onto the carpeted floor, feeling the burn of the synthetic material as he skidded to a stop. Hawk rolled and opened fire, emptying the magazine.

The ejector locked back, and he tossed the AK aside. Then he drew his Glock and fired half a magazine before scrambling to his feet once more.

"Frigging bastards."

Hawk crawled out onto the other landing before standing up and pressing his back against the wall.

He poked the Glock around the opening and fired the rest of the magazine along the hallway.

When the magazine was empty, he dropped it out and reloaded.

Sudden shouts emanating from the courtyard below reached up to him. Hawk tentatively looked down and saw more armed men running across the paved area. "Shit, Jake, this is a load of bollocks."

He raised the Glock and fired at the shooters below, making them scatter for cover. But it wasn't long before their gunfire erupted, sending him lurching back.

Hawk fired again and turned to run along the balcony, but the problem he had was that all roads led to Rome. And Rome was currently occupied by the enemy. Now he was trapped on a level with shooters coming at him from two sides.

The Talon operator reached the end of the balcony where it turned to the right. Looking back, Hawk saw shooters emerge from the hallway. He ducked down into cover and fired three shots. One of the intruders cried out and fell.

It didn't help the situation much. Hawk was still trapped between two assaulting forces. He rose once more and opened fire. Another magazine emptied and he dropped back down to reload. Patting his pockets for another magazine, realization dawned that he'd made a grave mistake. He was out of ammunition.

"Dumb, stupid frigging rookie error that was," Hawk growled.

He tossed the Glock on the balcony beside him. There was only one thing he could do. He raised his hands and stood up, praying that they wouldn't shoot him.

CHAPTER THIRTEEN

Belgrade, Serbia

"WHERE THE HELL IS HE?" Anja snapped. "He should have been here by now."

"What do you want me to do?" Gray asked.

"We give him another couple of minutes and then we go."

"We're going to leave him?"

"That is exactly what we're going to do. Jake is a big boy. He will find us."

"Shit."

Anja looked at her watch once more. The team was exposed, and she didn't like it. They should have been out of there minutes ago. Sudden gunfire erupted and bullets stitched a line along the side of the van. "Go! Go! Go!" she shouted.

Gray stomped on the gas and the rear wheels of the vehicle spun. It shot forward out into an alley and then he swung hard right on the wheel. Its rear end skipped across the pavement before it straightened with a little correction of the steering wheel. Then the motor roared as it shot towards the end of the alley and the street beyond.

When they reached the intersection, Gray swung left. Once again, the rear end fishtailed and then straightened, just missing an oncoming vehicle.

"Where do we go?" Gray asked Anja.

"Just drive and let me think."

A few heartbeats later, she retrieved the cell in her pocket, dialed a number and waited. When the connection was made, a person answered. Their voice was British, but it wasn't Hawk.

"Hello, love."

Anja frowned. "Who is this?"

"Who are you?" the voice asked.

"Let me speak to Jake."

"Poor old Jake is a little bit busy about now. He's getting to know the chaps."

More thoughts ran through Anja's mind as she tried to place the voice. Then it came to her. "Boyle?"

"That's right, love. Looks like you win. Or maybe I do 'cause I'm the one that's got Jake here."

"Let me speak to him."

"I don't think so. You see, we might just hang on to him until a little matter of $50 million is settled. What do you think?"

"I think maybe we can come to some arrangement," Anja replied.

"That's just what I hoped you would say," Boyle said. "But get this. You have 24 hours to have it back where it should be. After that I start cutting pieces off your boy here. Understood?"

"Yes, I understand. Now, you understand this. If I don't get Jake back in one piece, I'm going to come after you. And then I'm going to start cutting pieces off you. Starting with your dick."

There was a chuckle on the other end. Then she heard him say, "I like you. It's a shame you're going to have to die."

"Let's just settle for one thing at a time, shall we? When and where?"

"Just as soon as you're ready to do it, love. Transfer the money back, we'll let your boy go."

"I don't think so. We have a meeting face to face. We do the transfer and the exchange then. 10:00 o'clock tomorrow morning."

"Fine. I don't much care when. Just as long as the money comes back to the boss. Where do you want to do it?"

Anja thought for a moment. "There is an old cement works on the West side of Belgrade. We'll do it there."

The line disconnected and Anja looked at Gray. "We have some planning to do."

———

HAWK LOOKED AT BOYLE. "I guess what they said was true, huh?"

"What's that, Jake?"

"That you would work for anyone."

"Money is money."

"You know these people are slavers?"

"Doesn't concern me."

"It should. Working for them will get you killed."

"Says he who is staring down the barrel," Boyle shot back at him.

"Don't say you weren't warned."

A door opened and Novak appeared. "Everything will be ready for in the morning."

There was a concerned look on her face.

"What is wrong?" Boyle asked.

"I think it is odd that they have picked a time that is covered by daylight hours instead of night."

"Maybe they want to see what's coming."

"Shame you won't," Hawk said.

"Shut up, Jake, or I'll give you a few more lumps."

"Just saying."

Boyle glared at him. He turned his attention back to Novak. "We'll have men on location. Don't worry."

"I think I will," she replied. "Until this is over. This has cost my boss a lot of money and drawn a lot of attention from outside sources."

Hawk chuckled. "I heard Noskov had men in the city."

It was her turn to glare at the Talon operative. "Would you like us to gag you?"

Boyle frowned. "How did you know Noskov had men in the city?"

"Because I was there when they killed Desarae Peeters. She wanted me to kill him."

"Why you?"

"Because I'm good at what I do. Now you know."

"Did you sleep with her?" Novak asked. There seemed to be a hint of jealousy in her tone.

"No, I'm pretty particular about those I dip my wick in."

She rolled her eyes. "I've had enough of this fool. Come with me, Lester. We need to go over it again."

Hawk smiled once more. "You've got a right to be worried. They're coming to get you."

Boyle shook his head. "Shut up, Jake."

Hawk's grin widened, opening the cut in his bottom lip. He'd seen the look in Boyle's eyes, and the man was worried.

———

THE COMBAT KNIFE drove between the ribs of the guard and into his heart, stopping it midbeat. To make sure of the man's death, Gray withdrew it, using it to open the throat.

He lowered the man to the damp ground, wiped the glistening blade, replaced it into the sheath on his hip, and brought the suppressed AK-12 back up to his shoulder. "X-Ray neutralized."

"Copy," Anja replied.

She had taken up a position where she could cover Gray's infiltration with the Dragunov rifle she was using.

Gray moved again across the grounds of Amsel Haus towards the rear entrance. So far, he'd taken down two guards and there was another walking the perimeter of the house itself.

Gray crouched behind a hedge and waited for him to come back around. He could hear his heartbeat in his ears and slowed his breathing to bring it down. Over his comms he heard Anja say, "X-Ray spotted. Ten meters and closing."

The Brit remained silent. He lowered the AK and let it hang by its strap. He reached once more for his knife as Anja said, "Five meters."

Gray adjusted his grip.

"Three meters."

His muscles tensed like a coiled cobra ready to strike.

"One meter."

Footsteps.

"Execute, execute."

Gray came up from behind the hedge like a wraith from the abyss. Once more his knife did its gruesome work and another guard crossed over into the great beyond.

The Brit dragged the body behind a large greenhouse and reached for his AK. "Moving to the house."

"Copy."

Karl spoke for the first time. He had set up in the van they would use for exfil. "ISR has multiple signatures

154

throughout the house. Where Jake is I've no idea. You'll need someone to talk."

"Great."

"Be careful, Marcus. I've tagged at least two government ministers who passed through the doors this evening and, get this, Mikhail Markov."

"Who is Mikhail Markov?" Gray asked.

"Russian oligarch. Worth billions and travels with a heavily armed entourage."

"Where are they?"

"A couple went inside; the rest are with the cars out front."

"So the number of X-Rays just grew?"

"Affirmative."

"Thanks for the heads up."

"I was keeping it as a surprise."

"Have you got their security feed on loop?"

"You're right to go—hold, hold, hold."

"What's happening?" Gray asked.

"I've got an X-Ray who has just emerged from the rear door."

"Ma'am, do the honors."

"Sending."

As Gray moved once more, he emerged from behind the greenhouse then turned towards the house only meters away. He heard the passage of the bullet from the Dragunov and the thump of the impact. The target crumpled to the ground in a tangle of arms and legs.

Gray stepped over him and tried the door. It opened silently and he slipped inside.

The lights in the kitchen were on and it was clear. Moving to a doorway, he peered along a short hallway which joined a T-junction at the end. He was just about to step out when a man appeared coming his way. He was black and wearing a suit.

Gray ducked back and waited patiently for him to

155

appear. When he did, the Brit hurriedly subdued him using his hand clamped over his mouth and the tip of his knife pricking the flesh at his throat.

"Just keep quiet and you'll be fine, understood?"

The man nodded.

"Good. Where is the prisoner?"

"I—I—" he faltered.

"Take your time, just tell me where he is."

"U—upstairs. Last door on the right."

Gray nodded. "Now, just go outside and stare at the stars for a while. Don't come back in."

"O—okay."

"If you come back, I will kill you," the Brit cautioned him.

"I not come back."

Gray let him go and hoped it wasn't a choice he would regret.

As he turned to move along the hallway, the black man stopped him. "Not that way."

"What?"

"Come with me."

The man took Gray across the kitchen to a small doorway. He opened it to reveal a narrow staircase with a steep incline. "This way."

At the top of the stairs Gray found a closed door. Cracking it open, he peered through the slit to ensure all was clear on the other side before stepping out into the hallway and making the short journey towards the end.

When he was almost there, a noise at the end behind him signaled the arrival of two people. A man and a woman. With nowhere to go, Gray opened the nearest door and stepped through.

Years of training had taught him to consciously clear every room he entered. It wasn't long before he ascertained that he wasn't alone. Standing beside a large bed was a slender black woman dressed it a frilly red corset.

Her eyes widened as though she was about to scream.

"Don't," Gray said. "You'll get us both killed."

"Why would they kill me?"

"Death by association."

"Who are you?"

"Wait. I'll explain in a moment."

Gray listened near the door and once it was quiet, he turned and said, "I'm here for the bloke they have prisoner at the end of the hallway."

"I know the man you seek."

"Is he alright?"

"I think so." Her accent was heavy. "You didn't say who you were."

"I'm—I'm here to get my friend."

"Marcus, what is happening?"

"Just a moment, boss."

The woman frowned. "Who are you talking to?"

"My boss."

"Where is he?"

"She's nearby."

Suddenly the woman looked hopeful. "Can you get us out?"

Gray shook his head. "Not yet. But we're working on it."

"You have to help us."

"We will, just not tonight."

"If you don't get me out of here, I'll scream."

"Shit. Wait here. I'll be back."

"Take me with you."

Gray sighed. "I can't. It's too dangerous."

The woman suddenly grew angry and tore at her corset. It came free and exposed firm breasts which shook with her movements. Before the Brit could look away, she turned and showed him the crisscross scars on her back. "It is too dangerous to stay," she hissed.

The sight only made things worse. "Get dressed and wait here. I'll be back."

Through arguing, he exited the room and walked into a guard who was traversing the hallway.

"Shit, bollocks!" the man exclaimed.

"Got that right," Gray said and hit him hard in the throat.

The man fell and the Brit took out his knife and plunged it down into his chest, silencing him.

But it didn't stop there. A door opened and a woman saw the body, saw the knife, and screamed. Her position in the doorway was suddenly taken by a larger man with a bulbous nose. He took one look at Gray and started shouting in Russian.

"Fuck a duck." He fired the AK and a line of bullet holes appeared across the semi naked Russian's chest. "Alpha, I think I just killed the oligarch chap."

"Just find Jake and get out," Anja said.

"I'm working on it."

Not worrying about trying the door, Gray just kicked it and with the sound of splintering wood, it flew back

Light from the hallway filled the room and he saw Hawk sitting tied to a chair. "About time you got here."

"Been busy. Boss, I've got our friend."

"Roger."

Gray began to untie him, handing Hawk the Glock he was carrying. Then he said, "Follow me."

Upon entering the hallway, two large men in suits appeared with handguns. The suppressed AK fired, and both slumped to the carpeted floor. Hawk noticed the dead Russian on the floor in front of them. "Who's he?"

"Rich Russian bloke. I'll tell you later."

"Rich?"

"Billionaire."

"Oh boy. Someone is going to be pissed."

"Yeah, maybe. In here."

"What are you doing?" Hawk growled, confused.

In the room, they found the woman waiting. She was dressed. "I didn't think you would come back."

"I said I would," Gray replied.

"What's going on, Mucker?" Hawk asked.

"She's coming with us."

"Be fucked."

"I don't have time to argue, Jake."

"Shit."

"Let's get out of here," Gray said.

Hawk moved to the door and peered out to see more men approaching. He raised the Glock and opened fire. Blowing off four rounds, he ducked back into the room. "We're going out the window."

Gray went over to it and flipped the latch. Pushing on it he leaned out, looking down. "There could have been a pool there."

"What do we have, Marcus?"

"Bushes."

"Better than nothing. Out you go."

Gray climbed through the window and disappeared. Hawk looked at the woman. "If you're coming with us, then you'd better get moving."

She looked towards the window. "Out there?"

"You can stay if you want to, love, but either way, we're going."

"Have mercy."

The woman looked out through the window and hesitated. Meanwhile a burst of gunfire shredded the door. Hawk opened fire, the Glock's bullets punching through the thin veneer. "Make up your fucking mind or get out of the way," Hawk snarled. "I'm not dying in here because you can't make up your bloody mind."

Again, she hesitated.

"Stuff this for a game of marbles," Hawk muttered and ran over to her.

Before she knew it, the woman was scooped up in the Talon man's arms and thrown out of the window. Then he followed her out, just as the door caved in.

Hawk picked himself up and heard Gray say, "The window, boss, can you see it?"

"No."

"Shit."

Gunfire rattled and the garden and bushes all around them came alive with deathly movement. Hawk grabbed the woman by the arm and thrust her forward. "Move!"

Bullets chased them out of the garden from the window above.

Gray turned the corner of the building and almost ran headlong into a guard. Instinctively he reached for his knife and brought it out in a slashing motion. The razor-sharp blade opened the man's clothing and flesh beneath it. The guard reeled back as he tried to evade the swipe, but Gray followed him. A second cut opened the man's throat. Blood sprayed as the man fell back, grabbing at the ghastly wound, trying to keep himself alive.

"This way," Gray called over to Hawk.

The dead guard had been armed with an MP5 which Hawk picked up. He then followed Gray and the woman as he kept an eye on their six.

In Gray's ear, Anja said, "Keep moving. This place is coming alive."

"That's the plan, boss."

"Damn! Hold fast!"

Gray went to ground, taking the woman with him. Hawk needed no instruction. The crack of a high-powered bullet passed close. A cry of pain was followed by another shot.

"You're clear," Anja said.

"Come on, Jake, and...you."

"My name is Akin. I'm from Nigeria."

"Keep moving, Akin," Gray said. "We're almost there."

Moments later they reached the perimeter fence and then found themselves on the other side. They climbed into the awaiting van and Karl's head whipped around. "Who is she?"

"Hello, Jake, good to see you," Hawk said with sarcasm.

"Her name is Akin," Gray supplied. "She decided to leave."

The door opened once more, and Anja climbed in. She glanced at Akin and said, "Who is she?"

"I'm fine, thanks, boss," Hawk said as the van lurched forward.

"Her name is Akin. She was a slave there, and she wanted out, so I brought her along."

"And what do we do with her?" Anja's voice was sharp, whiplike.

"I don't fucking know, boss, but anywhere is better than there."

"I hope you're right. I'll organize for her to be taken to the embassy where she can be questioned by Interpol."

"I do not want to be any trouble," Akin said.

"You won't be," Anja told her. "In fact, despite going off book, Gray might have done some good. But we'll have to act fast."

"Which embassy, boss?" Gray asked.

"The British. I'll have them pick her up from the new digs."

"The what?"

"Our new residence."

"We need to get Ilse out of the hospital," Hawk said. "Get her back to home."

"One step ahead of you," Anja said. "She's back where we've set up."

"But who is looking after her?"

"I got someone from the embassy on loan."

"Good."

"So, right now we need to regroup and work out our next step."

"Getting out of Serbia would be a good step," Hawk said.

"Not yet. We've still got work to do."

"Shit."

CHAPTER FOURTEEN

Belgrade, Serbia

THE HUG LASTED a little longer than was necessary, but Hawk didn't mind. When he eventually let Ilse go, he took a step back and stared at her face. It was pale and drawn and she looked weak. "You need to sit down," he told her.

"I've been laying down forever. The exercise will do me good. Make me stronger."

"Just remember, it wasn't that long ago you almost died."

"I'm well aware of that fact." She stared at him for a moment and moved her head closer to his. "We need to talk."

He wanted to pull away from her, to walk out of the room to avoid the conversation she wanted to have with him but knew he couldn't. "Yeah, I guess we do."

"Tell me you haven't felt it."

"I've tried not to."

"But you have."

He shifted uncomfortably but Ilse's hands on his narrow hips steadied him. "Don't, Jake."

163

"Ilse, I—"

"Don't, Jake," she whispered.

"You're not going to kiss me, are you?"

"Maybe."

"What would my wife say?"

Ilse smiled, almost tiredly. "I don't care."

Their bodies molded together, and her lips were just about to touch his when the door opened. "I hope I'm not interrupting anything?" Anja asked.

"Ilse stumbled," Hawk lied.

"Yes, on her feet too much. However, we have another mission to prep for, but before we get to it, I need someone to take Ilse to the airport. Global will have a jet and a doctor and nurse there when she arrives."

"I can do that," Hawk said.

Anja shook her head. "No, Marcus can. I need you here."

He glanced at Ilse who gave him an almost imperceptible nod.

Hawk looked at Anja. "Fine."

"When do I leave?" Ilse asked.

"In twenty minutes."

"Okay."

"Can I have a word, Ilse?" She stared at Hawk while she spoke.

"I'll go and find something to do," he said.

After he had left the room and was out of earshot, Anja paused before saying, "What is going on between you and Jacob?"

"Not much."

"It didn't look like not much," the Talon leader replied.

"It has only just surfaced, Miss Meyer."

"No, no more Miss Meyer. We've been through too much."

"Fine."

Anja sighed. "Work out what it is. I don't like it, and if it interferes with your work, I'll transfer one or both of you out of here so fast—"

"I already told you—"

"I know what you said, Ilse. Now go away and think about it. We deal in life and death, and hesitation could mean the latter if something happens in the field. I need you to be sure that it's not going to do that. Understood?"

"Yes, ma'am."

"God knows I should transfer one of you right now," Anja said. "Just get it sorted."

"Yes, boss."

"Thank you. That's all I'll say on the matter. Now, go back to Hereford and mend. And don't forget to say goodbye to everyone."

To Jake, you mean?

———

"JAKE?"

He turned and saw her standing there. "You ready?"

Ilse nodded. "Yes."

"What did the boss say?"

"She asked me what this is?" Ilse replied, pointing a finger between them both.

"What did you tell her?"

"I told her the truth. That I didn't know what it was, and it had just surfaced."

"How did she take it?"

"She wants me to think about it, be sure before I go and fuck her team up," Ilse said bitterly.

"Whoa, what's with that?" Hawk asked.

"I'm angry, Jake. Angry that you know how I feel but you haven't said once how you feel about me. I know we work together, and it could be as dangerous as hell. But I can't help how I feel."

He nodded. "You're right, it could be dangerous, and I don't know how I would react in the field if something happened and you were with me. But I want to find out."

Ilse smiled, the bitterness gone.

"But," he continued, "we need to be sure. The boss is right. You need to think hard about it. I'm dangerous, Ilse, and that is what the boss is worried about. I'm not about to change how I operate. I start mucking around with that and it could get me killed. And yes, the way I operate could get me killed anyway but I'd rather go out fighting for the greater good than withering away in some old people's home. You need to know you can accept that fact."

He was right and she knew it. Ilse nodded. "You forget that I'm part of this world, too, Jake. I understand the dangers more than other women would."

"I accept that."

She stared at him. "All right, Jake, I'll think about it, but I need to know, that if I decide that I want to do this, will you still be there?"

"If you can accept that then I will be willing."

Ilse smiled and stepped forward. He took her in his arms and felt the warmth of her body filter through his clothing. "You take care, Ilse. Get better, I need you giving me orders."

She kissed him gently on the cheek. "I'll see you when you get to Hereford. Stay safe."

He gave her a wry smile. "You know me. Besides, they gave me a new bulletproof bodysuit."

"How is it?"

"Frigging hurts when you get shot."

Ilse giggled

———

"WE HAVE A PROBLEM," Anja said as they sat down around the table for the briefing.

"We've always got problems," Hawk said dabbing a bruise on his face with his finger. "When we're not going into trouble, people are trying to kill us. I'm starting to think that my career change was hasty."

"Well, it's about to become even more dangerous," Anja interjected.

"Sounds ominous."

"The girl you got out of Amsel Haus—"

"Akin?"

"Yes, Akin. The Brits were moving her to a safe location—"

"Sorry, boss," Gray interrupted. "But where is safer than the embassy?"

"I don't know. I asked and they refused to answer. But we're getting off the beaten path. They were shifting her, and the transport was hit. Everyone in it was killed except the girl."

"They took her back to the house?" Hawk asked.

"No, the German embassy."

Hawk was puzzled. "Why would they do that?"

"Hermann is there," Anja said. "We wanted to bring him to Serbia, well, we succeeded."

"He'll be questioning her about us," Gray surmised.

"Most probably," Anja agreed. "We need to work out where we go from here. I'm open to suggestions."

There was a moment of silence before Hawk asked. "How corrupt are the coppers here?"

"Some not all."

"What about Interpol?"

"The ones we've worked with are square," Karl said.

"How much do we have on him?"

"Everything we have is recorded, as you know, so we've got those bank accounts, witnesses."

"Is it enough for them to make a case?"

"Let's find out," Anja said. "Karl, sift through the intel we have. I'll make a call to Lyon."

———

HAWK STUDIED the two Interpol officers sitting opposite him. One call and within twenty-four hours they were in Belgrade. Not that they didn't already have them there, but these were target specific. One, Guy Fontaine, was in command of European Organized Crime, the other, Collette Moreau, European Sex Trafficking and Slavery. Hawk put them both in their late thirties. Fontaine was dressed in a suit and had tight cropped dark hair and a solid build. Moreau was slender, athletic, possibly because she worked out at least four days a week. Her dark hair was tied back to reveal fine features. Her attire was different. Jeans, cotton shirt, and a coat which was removed, revealing a shoulder holster with a Glock resting in it.

"It is good to finally meet in person," Moreau said. "What you have been doing to the sex trafficking world has been welcome."

"We still have a way to go yet," Anja said. "But, yes, it is good to meet you face to face as well, instead of virtually."

Moreau nodded. "Yes, once we are rid of Ilya Noskov the world will be a better place."

"It may be closer than you think."

The Interpol officer gave her a quizzical look but left it at that.

"What can we help you with, Miss Meyer?" Fontaine asked.

"Anja, please."

"Anja."

"I would like to show you something to see what you

make of it. We have an operation in progress but before we go any further, we would like your opinion."

"Opinion on what?" Moreau asked.

"Whether we capture or kill the German Minister of Defense," Hawk said without blinking.

The two officers stared at him and waited for him to smile. It wasn't forthcoming. Fontaine raised his eyebrows and rubbed his chin, his five o'clock shadow making a scratching noise on his hand. "You're serious."

"As a funeral, mate. The bloke needs taking off the board or being put down. However—"

Anja cut him off. "However, if we can give you enough evidence and deliver him to you, then it would save a lot of trouble."

"You are talking about Wolfgang Hermann, right?" Moreau asked.

Hawk said, "That's right. Is he on your radar?"

"Has been for a while. But being a politician in a foreign country, it makes things difficult."

"The prick is a modern-day slaver," Hawk growled.

"Jacob," Anja cautioned him.

"Sorry, boss."

"We hear you," Fontaine said. "But we can't touch him without special dispensation. We won't get that because the German government won't allow him to be extradited. It would be too embarrassing for them."

"What if we could give him to you?"

"How legal would it be?" Moreau asked.

"Possibly not very, but you won't have to extradite him. He'll just fall into your lap."

"You would have to get him out of Germany," Fontaine pointed out.

"He's not in Germany," Anja said.

They stared at her.

"He's here in Belgrade at the embassy."

"That might as well be Germany," Moreau pointed out.

Hawk said, "We'll get him; you be ready."

"You seem to be forgetting one thing," Moreau pointed out. "We need evidence if we are to convict. A lot more than what we have."

"Raid his slave brothel."

"We can't. Belgrade justice system keeps denying us what we need."

Anja pushed a folder across the table. Moreau opened it and looked at the contents. She picked up a thumb drive. Anja said, "Recordings of radio transmissions as well as electronic pages of evidence. The sheets are hard-copies. You'll also find photos in there as well."

"You're giving this to us?" Fontaine asked uncertainly, looking back and forth from the file to Anja.

"Yes. Look over it and make an informed decision. Once we know what we're doing then we have one more mission to carry out."

Moreau stared at Anja's stoic face. "Noskov, isn't it?"

"Maybe."

"You know where he is?"

"Not for certain."

"What are your plans?"

"To end it."

Moreau let the rest go. "Give us an hour to look over this stuff and we'll let you know."

Anja nodded. "We'll leave you with it. There is one more thing for you to think on. Did you know he was actually Jonas Sauer?"

From their reaction, they didn't.

Moreau went through everything, talked, looked, and talked some more. Two hours later they were all gathered once more. Moreau said, "Between what we have, and what you have, we could do this. Tell me your plan."

Anja looked at Hawk. "Jake?"

"We take him off the street."

"Kidnap him?" Fontaine asked.

"It's either that or storm the embassy. Not something I would suggest."

"He'll have bodyguards."

Hawk looked at Anja. She nodded and said, "Hermann doesn't use state-sanctioned bodyguards. Those that he uses are from a private security company. From the intel we've been able to gather in the brief amount of time we've had, they are mercenaries for hire, nothing more. Jake and Marcus will be cleared to use all force necessary to secure the package."

"Lethal force?" Moreau said.

"Yes."

Moreau and Fontaine glanced at each other. Fontaine said, "We should wash our hands of it right now. It's just straight out illegal."

"But what we don't know," Moreau said, "can't hurt us."

"Once we have him secured, we'll reach out."

"Just one question," Moreau asked. "I know I shouldn't. What if it all goes sideways?"

Hawk grinned. "Then we fight like hell until they're all dead or we are."

———

"WE NEED TO DRAW HIM OUT," Anja said to the rest of her people. "Any ideas?"

"We could always just ask him," Hawk said.

Gray grinned. "Yeah, I'm sure he'd just say yes and come out and play."

"I might know of a way," Karl said. "I'd need a few hours to set it up, but it might work."

"Do it," said Anja. "I trust you."

So he went to work on his plan, and when he was

finished he brought Anja a thumb drive. She held it up in front of her and asked, "What is it?"

"You'll have to watch it."

She plugged it in and tapped a few keys before the USB started to work. She watched what was on it before looking at her tech. "That's good work."

"I just hope it's enough," Karl said.

"Shall we find out?"

Three hours later a small package was delivered to Wolfgang Hermann at the German embassy. He frowned and looked up at the young man who had placed it in front of him. "Has it been scanned?"

"Yes, sir. It looks to be a small drive of some kind."

"All right, leave me and I will look at it."

Hermann opened the envelope and tipped it up. A small thumb drive fell onto the desk, and he picked it up, studying the device. He plugged it into the computer in front of him and watched as it started.

The German MP frowned. It was a movie—of him, yet it couldn't be him. He was naked on a bed, reaching out for something—for someone out of shot. Then they appeared and he felt his revulsion rise. It was a woman. A black woman, and she, too, was naked.

As he watched she joined him, embracing, kissing. He bit her breasts and she reacted passionately, arching her back, thrusting her chest forward.

Next, he rolled on top of her, thrusting forward, the woman's legs wrapping around him as she met the vigorous stroke.

Suddenly the movie stopped, and a woman's face filled the screen. "Hello, Wolfgang. Or should I say, Jonas? I'm guessing you'll know my face but if you don't, it's Anja Meyer. Formerly of German intelligence, but now I lead Taskforce Talon. I'm guessing you watched yourself in the feature. You can keep this one, we have others. I plan on releasing them to the BBC and other European news networks unless we can make some kind of deal. I'll be in touch."

Hermann felt his ire rise sharply. But not just that, he also felt the revulsion threaten to burst loose. There was the other fact. They knew he was Jonas Sauer. And that could not stand.

His cell buzzed in his pocket. Not the private one, the other; the one he kept for business. "Yes?"

"Hello, Jonas, did you enjoy the show?"

"You?"

"Yes, who else were you expecting? Natalija Novak? Oh, by the way, thanks for the donation. Our funding has been rather short of late."

"It was you who stole my money?" he asked incredulously.

"Would you like it back?"

"What kind of a stupid question is that?"

"I tell you what, come on out and we'll make a trade."

"What trade?" he asked cautiously.

"You have a woman in your custody. We want her back."

"You are willing to trade fifty million for a Darkie?"

"We kind of became attached to her."

"Where?"

"The old cement works on the far side of Belgrade."

"Fine, when?"

"Tomorrow night. Ten o'clock."

"I will be there."

———

THE CALL DISCONNECTED and Anja looked at Hawk. "He's taken the bait."

"We'd better get ready then."

"You realize that if this goes wrong, we're done."

Hawk gave her a weird grin. "Not done, boss, dead."

173

"Will you have sufficient time to plan?"

Hawk nodded. "Yeah, I'll get it done. I might need some money though to grease a few palms."

"Cash?" Anja asked.

"Always the best language."

"I'll see that you get it."

CHAPTER FIFTEEN

Belgrade, Serbia

"TALK TO ME, KARL," Hawk said in a low voice.

"ISR is up and running, Jake. Elvis has left the building."

"Shit a brick," Hawk said with a low chuckle. "I'd shelve that one, mate."

"You don't like it?"

"Terrible. What do you see?"

"Three vehicles. SUVs, in line, just coming up to speed."

"How are the roadblocks looking?"

"Fine. I don't know how you managed it, but everything looks to be in place."

"I do," Anja muttered. "Our account is two-million lighter."

"Money makes the world go around, boss," Hawk said.

"Not that much."

"It worked."

"Remains to be seen."

"If you two have finished, I have something else for you," Karl said, interrupting the back and forth.

"Speak to me, clean one," Hawk urged.

"Not funny, Jake."

"Just tell me what the issue is."

"Three shadow vehicles have just appeared. Again, they are SUVs, and my estimate would be twelve X-Rays total."

"Don't you just love it when the bad guys do shit like this?" Hawk growled.

"What do you want to do, Jake?" Anja asked.

"Marcus?"

"I'd say the numbers are just about even, Jake," Gray replied.

"My thoughts exactly."

Hawk gripped the steering wheel of the BMW he'd acquired for the mission. It was dark blue and one of the newer models which pleased Anja no end. "It comes back in one piece, Jacob," she'd insisted. "Not even a scratch. Spending that much money on a vehicle is ludicrous."

"Built for a fast getaway, boss."

"One piece, Jake."

So now he waited, beside him in the passenger seat was an M72A9 Rocket Launcher. Just what he needed to stop an armored vehicle.

"Sitrep," Hawk said.

"The three SUVs are still shadowing at a distance of around 1000 meters," Karl said. "The diversions are working. They should be on you within two minutes."

Hawk was satisfied with the response. He'd chosen the location because of its proximity to the embassy. There was less chance of any deviations that way, as there would have been with a long transit. He started the BMW. "Are you ready, Marcus?"

"Just say when, good buddy,"

"Good grief."

The time passed slowly with updates from Karl. The plan was to hit the small convoy, and load Hermann into the BMW before taking him to the nearest airfield with the capability of servicing a small jet. This would be Talon's point of departure as well.

"Sixty seconds, Jake," Karl said.

"We go on thirty. Just have that plane ready." He pulled a black ski mask over his head.

The seconds passed by slowly, painfully. Until Karl said, "Thirty seconds, Jake."

The BMW was already in gear when Hawk pushed the pedal to the floor. The wheels screeched as it leapt forward onto the main street. He slammed on the brakes and climbed out of the vehicle, taking the rocket launcher with him. He extended the tube, brought it up to his shoulder, ready to fire as the headlights in front of him grew larger.

Then he fired.

The impact of the rocket seemed to throw the front of the lead vehicle into the air. An orange ball of flame lit the street and the buildings surrounding it. Behind the disintegrating vehicle, the other two stopped. As soon as the tires became stationary that was Gray's cue to commit.

Out of the alley in the right position came a large garbage truck. The giant metal monster slammed into the side of the trailing SUV, driving it across the street into a building on the other side.

Gray reversed and stopped in the middle of the street, blocking the thoroughfare. He jumped down from the truck with an AK-12 up, sweeping the area for threats.

Taking the same type of weapon from the BMW, Hawk moved towards the remaining SUV. The passenger's front door flew open and an armed man stepped out of the vehicle. Hawk dropped him with two well placed rounds.

The driver's side door opened next. The driver, however, didn't produce a weapon, but remained hunkered down behind the vehicle's engine block for protection. A fatal error on his part was failing to check his rear. When he eventually did come up to fire, Gray shot him in the back of the head.

"Jake, the shadowing vehicles have sped up," Karl said over the comms. "You need to get the package and get out now."

"We're working on it."

There were still two men in the SUV illuminated by the one burning in front of it. Hawk and Gray approached from opposite directions. "Neutralize the threat, Marcus."

"I would if I could see what the threat was," he shot back.

Hawk opened fire with the AK, bullets hammering the front of the SUV. Suddenly the rear right door flew open, and a man exploded from it firing an MP5.

Bullets cut through the air all around where Hawk stood. He calmly adjusted his aim with the AK and then squeezed the trigger. The man's head snapped back, and he collapsed like a marionette with its strings cut. "Get Hermann out now."

They approached the vehicle, Gray moving around to the remaining closed door. He opened it, then there sitting in the luxury seat, fear on his face, was Wolfgang Hermann.

Hawk said, "Alpha, we have the package. Moving to extract."

"Who are you?" demanded Hermann.

Both of the Talon operatives ignored the question. Gray zip-tied the minister's wrists together, and then put a black hood over his head.

Gray dragged Hermann from the vehicle and then along the street, past the burning SUV, towards the awaiting BMW.

"Jake, you need to take cover now!" the words from Karl were urgent. "You have X-Rays inbound. They're coming your way."

Hawk turned to look back over his shoulder and saw the approach of bouncing headlights. The screech of tires signaled what was about to happen. Every door flew open and twelve heavily armed men exited the vehicles.

Hawk's face turned to a sneer. "Shit, that'll fuck up your day. Marcus, contact rear. Take cover."

Which they did, just as the new arrivals started to open fire. And their only immediate cover was the BMW that Hawk had been ordered to bring back in one piece.

Bullets punched into the thin exterior of the vehicle, opening holes like it was a block of gelato.

"Boy, the boss is going to be pissed at you," Gray said, hunkered down beside Hawk.

"Just don't tell her," Hawk replied.

"You do know this is an open channel, don't you, Jacob?" Anja said.

"Forgot about that."

Beside them, Hermann flinched with every round impacting the BMW. It suddenly dawned on Hawk that they were firing at them without any regard to the safety of the German Defense Minister.

He ripped the hood from the man's head and stared hard at him as more bullets hammered into the vehicle. "Why are your men shooting at us like that?"

Beside Hawk, Gray rose and started letting off rounds with his AK. He managed to drop one of the assailants before being forced back down by the withering fire.

Hermann said something, but his voice was lost in the gunfire.

"What?" Hawk asked.

"I said they are not my men."

"Oh shit," Hawk said in resignation, replacing the hood. "Boss, the package has just confirmed that the X-Rays aren't his."

"Then, they must be Noskov's shooters."

"That would be my thinking."

Beside Hawk, Gray said, "Are you going to start shooting today? Tomorrow?"

The former SAS man came up over the hood and opened fire with the AK-12. Another of the shooters fell, but they were spread out wide and were pressing forward hard.

He dropped back down and said, "We need to get out of here."

"No shit."

Hawk grabbed Hermann by his collar and dragged him to his feet, all the while keeping him low. "Get up but keep your head down."

Gray rose once more and opened fire. "Go! Go!"

With the German defense minister in tow, Hawk ran towards the alley where he'd waited in the BMW. Bullets chased them all the way, grit caused by ricochets kicking up at their feet.

Once inside the alley mouth, Hawk slammed Herman against the wall. "Stay here. Move and I'll just shoot you."

The German remained still, shaking at the sound of gunfire. Meanwhile, Hawk slid along the wall of the building so he could support Gray. "Get ready to move, Marcus," he said into his comms.

The AK came up and he opened fire at a shooter crouched near the burning wreck of the first SUV. "Silly boy."

The AK-12 rattled to life and the shooter slumped sideways. "Move, Marcus."

Without once looking back, Gray was running towards the alley mouth. He almost made it when Hawk heard him snarl, "Ah, shit!"

He staggered but kept moving until he made the opening between the two buildings. Gray leaned against the wall beside Hawk. The former SAS man kept firing. "You all right, mucker?"

"Got hit in the arm."

"You wearing a suit?"

"Yeah, still bloody hurts though."

Hawk fired another burst. "Don't I know it. Alpha, we need a way out of here, right now."

Anja said, "We're working on it, Bravo."

Karl said, "Jake, head to the end of the alley. I'll have more by the time you get there."

Hawk looked at Gray. "Did you get that?"

"Roger."

"Take our friend and get moving. I'll be right behind you."

Gray moved toward Hermann and grabbed him. "Come on, cock. And don't give me any trouble; my arm still hurts."

They started along the alley while Hawk covered them. He fired some more shots before changing out the empty magazine. Once he reloaded, he fired some more rounds and began to run after Gray and Hermann.

"You'd better give me something Karl. Those pricks are right behind us."

"Once you get to the end of the alley, go left. The street is empty, and there is foliage to cover your exfil route."

"Copy. Marcus, go left."

"I can't believe you lost another damn car, Jake," Anja muttered.

"If it makes you feel any better it didn't actually cost anything."

"Shit."

As they turned the corner it was obvious what Karl had been talking about. The street was lined with trees and bushes on both sides, limiting the range of illumination thrown by the streetlamps. They moved quickly, Gray pushing Hermann.

"Speak to me, Karl," Hawk said as they went forward.

"Cross over."

They deviated and rushed across the street. Behind them they could hear the voices in the alley.

Once on the other side they kept going.

"Jake, on your right you'll see a driveway."

"Got it."

"Go down it."

"Where does it go?" Hawk asked.

"You should be able to cut through to the next street over. Be aware there is pedestrian traffic on it."

"Just what we need," he muttered.

The drive was concrete and took them down alongside a two-floor brick building. There was no outdoor lighting which helped mostly. When they got to the back, however, they found a wooden fence blocking their path.

"Hold it, Marcus, I'll make a hole."

Hawk kicked the paling fence and made a hole in it big enough for them to climb through. On the other side, the former SAS man stopped abruptly. Out of the shadows and into the dim moonlight emerged seven figures to block their path.

Hawk stopped, Gray and the hooded Hermann behind him. One of the figures stepped forward and said something in Serbian.

I don't have time for this shit. "We're just passing through, mate."

"English?" The voice was heavily accented. "What are you doing with the man you have there?"

"Not for you to worry about."

"But I think it is."

"You do realize that I'm holding a gun, right?"

"But there are many of us. We will kill you anyway."

Hawk grunted. "You won't, mate, you'll be down and fucking bleeding in the cobbles."

"We don't have time for this, Jake," Gray growled.

Sudden gunfire erupted from behind them, and bullets cracked close. Hawk spun as the gang members started moving in. He brought up the AK and opened fire at the wood fence, splintering it.

"Marcus, the building," Hawk snarled.

"It's a death trap," Gray said.

"Just move."

With gunfire loud in their ears, they ran towards the building. It was a tall apartment block, perhaps fourteen floors high.

They reached the door and found a chain through the handles but no hasp. Hawk dropped the chain and flicked on the flashlight attached to the AK-12 as he pushed through the door. It lit the foyer so they could see where they were going. The building was abandoned, evidenced by the graffiti and the smell.

"Where to?" Gray asked.

"Up?"

"They'll expect that."

"Then fuck it, we'll go down." He said into his comms, "Karl, do you still have a feed?"

"Lost you when you went inside," the tech replied.

"I need to know anything you can find out about this place."

"Bit late when you're already in there," Karl pointed out.

"We're going down. Find me a way out."

Anja came on the air. "Jake, I hope you know what you're doing."

"So do I. If we die down here blame Gray, it was his idea. I would appreciate it if you could muster some help."

"Sorry, Jake, I'll do what I can but for the moment you're on your own."

"Yeah, just about what I figured. Karl, find me a tunnel. Belgrade was renowned for them during the Second World War."

"I'll try."

They kept moving downward until they reached the

183

basement, which was a warren of empty rooms, except one that wasn't. It had a stack of boxes and crates in it. Always one to be curious, Hawk said, "Strange, what?"

"We don't have time, Jake."

Hawk ignored him and pushed one of the crates to the concrete floor so that it burst open. The contents spilled free and both men stared at the mess with admiration.

"Be stuffed," Gray said.

"I guess we know what those gangsters were up to."

"There's a lot of money there."

"I'd say they were guarding it for someone."

"Yeah, let's look around and see if we can find a way out."

Looking and listening was the order of the time. Looking for a way out, listening for their pursuers. "Hold," Hawk whispered.

Gray froze, ears straining. Against the far wall, Hermann moved, and Gray cat-footed it across to him, putting his mouth close to his ear. "You fuck this up and I'll kill you here."

Silence returned in a long pregnant pause. First there was nothing. Then came the sound of a soft soled boot crunching grit on concrete.

Hawk placed the AK on the concrete, leaving the flash-light on, and then reached for his knife. He crept across to the doorway that gave access into the basement room and pressed his back against the wall. Gray turned his light off. Whoever was out there knew they were there, but he saw no sense in giving them a second beacon to home in on.

As the shooter edged into the room, Hawk struck. Years of training showed in muscle memory and the knife struck with blinding speed, its last savage flick across the intruder's throat sending an outward spray of blood.

With fluid movements, Hawk let the body fall to the floor, releasing his knife to fall with it, drawing the Glock from his holster. He poked it around the corner of the doorway and fired three shots.

The noise was almost deafening in the concrete lined room, but didn't totally obliterate the cry of pain from the wounded man in the other room.

When nothing else happened, Hawk grabbed the AK and used the light to check both men.

"They're no more of a threat," he said. Then, "You found us a way out, Karl?"

"Yes, the way you came in."

"Aren't you a happy chap?"

"Sorry."

"All right, let's do this. Marcus, get our man."

Gray grabbed Hermann by the collar and dragged him to his feet. The minister still wore the hood and couldn't see what was happening. Taking point, Hawk started back through the basement rooms.

They started back up the stairs and had almost made it when gunfire rang out. Bullets ricocheted off the concrete stairwell, one hitting Hawk in his body armor. Just before he returned fire, however, he heard a grunt and saw Hermann buckle at the knees.

"This is just fucking great," he roared.

"He's gone, Jake," Gray responded.

"Motherfucker." He spoke into his comms, "Alpha, we've lost the package. The bastards have shot him."

"Say again, Bravo."

"I said he's dead."

"Roger, get out."

"Get out, she says," Hawk muttered. "What does she think we're doing? Having beer and nuts at the pub while we play darts?"

Gray performed a tactical reload and rammed home a fresh magazine. "Sounds good to me."

More rounds came down the stairwell.

Hawk said, "We've got one more flight and we're good. Ready?"

"Into the valley of death rode the two," Gray stated.

"Wasn't that meant to be six hundred?"

"Where the hell do you see six hundred?"

"Good point."

Hawk brought up his AK and started up.

———

THERE WAS a deathly silence filling the foyer. Gray limped while Hawk's left arm lay useless at his side, numb from taking a round. Around them lay dead men. Shooters from Medusa; Noskov's Medusa. They were a rabble, not trained well at all. Something Hawk was happy about.

He looked at Gray. "We need to have a word to whoever designed these Synoprathetic suits."

"Hurts like shit when you get shot," Gray said.

"Try getting shot in the chest then tell me how it feels."

"But we're still alive."

Sirens were sounding in the background. "Check some of these blokes before we get out of here."

A quick search turned up nothing of use and by then it was time to disappear. When the police did arrive, the two Talon men were gone.

CHAPTER SIXTEEN

Belgrade, Serbia

"I'D LIKE to say it was time to leave the country, but Interpol have asked for one last mission before we go," Anja said.

Hawk shook his head. "We need to be wheels up."

"I agree but Interpol has flagged a POI right here in the country."

Hawk looked sideways at Moreau. "We need to get out of this damn country. Especially after the op we just pulled went sideways."

"I wouldn't say it was a total loss," she replied.

"Tell that to the German government."

"You would be surprised."

Hawk sighed. "Who is the person of interest, anyway?"

Anja paused. "Lester Boyle."

"For crying out loud," Hawk growled.

"I told them we would do it."

The former SAS operative looked at Gray. "Of course, she did."

"We get him and get out."

"Boss, one does not just get Lester Boyle and get out. The bastard has nine lives like a cat. He doesn't get captured."

"They said dead or alive."

"This just gets fucking better. What did he do to get that tag?" Hawk asked.

"Interpol was running an operation in Warsaw, Poland. A pipeline was operating through there both ways. Girls were being funneled out of Russia, west, and from the west, into Russia. They set up a sting with Polish police and ran into an ambush. Boyle led it."

"So they want us to take a run at him," Hawk said.

"Yes."

"Fine, but once we're done, we go after Noskov. All in."

Anja nodded. "All in."

"Do you still have that Dragunov?"

"Yes."

"Then let's do it."

"WHO WOULD HAVE THOUGHT that someone like Boyle liked opera," Anja said in Hawk's ear.

Hawk grunted. "He doesn't. This is something else. Karl, keep an eye out."

"Like a hawk. Sorry, Jake."

Anja said, "They should be out in a few minutes. Keep an eye out and only shoot if the line of fire is clear."

The front of the opera house was lit with orange lighting which made the façade of the building look like something out of their world, almost haunting. Outside of that, dense shadows seemed to lurk everywhere. Then Hawk saw a shadow within a shadow. He paused his sweep and swung back.

"I've got an X-Ray at the eastern edge of the opera house hiding in the dark."

"Let me find out what I can see," Karl said. A few moments later he said, "I've got him. Can you see if he's armed or not?"

Hawk looked. "Hard to tell."

Anja said, "Bravo, look around and see if you can find any more."

Hawk swept the area again, this time with more care. "Shit, I've got another four. Someone is running an op. Karl, find out who is there in that building."

A few minutes later he came back. "This isn't good. I've found the name Ard Ulsens."

"Who is Ard Ulsens?"

"He runs Interpol's trafficking division."

Hawk was confused for a moment before his mind kicked in. "Dirty bastards. Fucking Interpol has set us up."

"What do you mean?" Anja asked.

"They knew. They knew Ulsens was going to be here, and they knew someone was going to make a play for him. Do we know for certain Boyle is in there?"

"We only operate on the intel. We haven't seen him."

"You need to find out if this is Boyle or Noskov."

"How could it be Noskov?" Karl asked. "You and Marcus took out his team."

"He's got more than one team. It's like—I don't know. What if their target first off was Hermann? Instead, we got to him first."

"That would explain why they weren't worried about hitting him."

"And now they go after Interpol's biggest asset, the one who makes life difficult for them."

"Why though?" Gray asked. "Why now?"

Another pregnant pause.

Hawk said, "Because he's all but found Noskov. Medvedev was good at hiding."

"But Noskov isn't Medvedev," Anja said.

"Exactly. Ulsens is getting too close. Medusa's armor is crumbling. Falling apart and Noskov is frequently forced to bring it out of the shadows. This is how we get him."

"But why kill Hermann?"

"I don't know but there has to be a link somewhere."

"Maybe it was something as simple as just knowing something he shouldn't have," Karl said.

"I have a bad feeling about this," Hawk said. "Boss, I advise you to move the asset."

"Now?"

"Yes."

"Karl, make the call."

"Yes, ma'am."

"Everyone on high alert," Anja said.

"Boss, I can't raise the secure facility."

"Damn it," she hissed. "Once the shooting starts, things are going to get chaotic. Targets of opportunity. But for Christ's sake, don't hit any civilians."

"Unlike us Noskov's men aren't going to take that advice," Hawk said.

"We don't even know if it is him, Jake."

"It's him, all right. He may not be here. But it's his men."

"I can hear a tone in your voice. Jake. You're about to propose something that isn't quite legal."

Hawk grunted. "The way I see it, boss, is we stop it before it starts. That means taking them out right now."

There was a pause before Anja spoke again. "All right, Jake. Stand by. Pick a target. Fire on my command."

Hawk and Gray settled in behind their weapons as they waited for Anja to give the word to open fire. It was going to be held up, but it would be better to ask for forgiveness than permission. And after all, Anja was the permission.

"Three, two, one, execute." Her voice was calm, calculated. Then, as her rifle slammed back into her shoulder, the other two opened fire.

The hidden men in the shadows danced violently as bullets struck their bodies. Within moments, three men were down and squirming on the hard concrete. Hawk shifted his aim and selected another watcher in the shadows. He squeezed the trigger on the AK-12 once more and felt the comforting recoil.

The target dropped. Hawk said into his mic, "Second X-Ray down. Karl, do we have many more targets out there?"

His question was answered for him within heartbeats as bullets sprayed his vantage point from the building close by. More shooters seemed to materialize from the surrounding darkness and joined the battle.

On top of the building to his left, Anja squeezed off another round from the Dragunov. The round punched into a shooter's chest and he flopped to the ground like a dead fish. Gray, on the other hand, suddenly found himself under intense fire and was pinned down.

"Bravo Two is taking heavy fire from the street. I can't move. They've got me pinned."

"Wait one, Bravo Two," said Hawk into his comms.

He searched the street and found where the fire was coming from. Three shooters had taken cover behind a vehicle and were now pouring fire upward towards the precipice where Gray was hidden.

The sights on the AK-12 snapped into line. Hawk stroked the trigger, and he felt the punch of the butt back into his shoulder. The first shooter went down sideways. Then the former SAS man flicked the fire selector around to auto. This time he held the trigger firmly back as the weapon chewed through the rest of the magazine, devouring what was in it within seconds.

Hawk said into his comms, "It should be clear now, Marcus."

"Thanks, Jake."

Within moments, things went from bad to worse as three black SUVs pulled up out front of the Opera House. Doors flew open as the vehicles released an additional eight shooters who quickly joined the battle.

"I think it's time to leave, boss," Hawk growled into his comms.

"I agree. Fall back. We'll meet at the rally point."

"Roger that."

Their rally point was an alley out the back where they'd left the van. Inside the van was Karl providing their mobile support. As he scanned his computer, he saw something approaching on ISR. "All field elements, be aware we have a helicopter coming in from the northeast."

"That can't be good," Hawk said.

"Give me a moment and I'll try to work out what it is."

Meanwhile, the team was falling back rapidly towards the rally point. The sound of gunshots echoed around the street.

"Holy crap," Karl breathed. "People, you've got a helicopter gunship on its way in. It's about one mike out. Move your asses. Sorry, boss."

By the time all three had reached the alley, the heavy beat of rotors could be heard echoing throughout the building-surrounded canyons.

"This is some heavy-duty backup," Hawk said as they climbed into the van. "Somehow I get the feeling this was a setup just for us."

Anja said. "How about we discuss this later? In the meantime, let's get the hell—"

She was unable to complete the sentence before bullets from a rotary cannon on the helicopter ripped up the alley outside. Some of the bullets punched into the van itself. "Out! Everyone get the fuck out!"

Doors opened and out they all tumbled into a new kind of hell. More bullets rained down from the sky. "Don't stop. Keep moving," Hawk shouted.

As they ran along the alley, volcanic eruptions seemed to spray from the asphalt behind them. Gray and Hawk dived to their left as a line of rounds caught up to them. From somewhere behind, a shout of pain could be heard. Hawk looked back from where he lay on the ground and saw the crumpled figure.

"Oh shit, no."

He scrambled back on all fours and then crouched over Karl. Blood was coming from the corner of his mouth and his chest heaved as he tried to draw in breath. He'd taken a round through his torso and it had blown most of his insides out. Hawk muttered a curse, looked on helplessly.

"I'm sorry, mate. There's not much I can do for you."

Karl tried to speak, but all he could manage was a cough, blood erupting from his lips. "We'll get him, mate. We'll bloody get him."

And with those words, Karl stopped breathing.

Hawk scooped up his computer and started running once more. Sensing something was wrong, Anja had stopped, and now she looked wide eyed at the former British SAS operator who ran towards her. "He's gone, boss. There's nothing we can do except stay alive."

"Oh, no."

Without hesitation, Hawk started pushing her along in front of him as they tried to escape the deathtrap that was the alley. "Keep moving. There's nothing more we can do."

"This way!"

Hawk looked to see Gray waving at them from a door to their left. "In here."

They changed their direction and ran through the

open doorway, following the former para. Once inside, they paused for a breath.

"We shouldn't have left him," Anja said.

"Boss, look at me."

Anja turned her face to look at Hawk in the dappled light. "There was nothing we could do for him. He's beyond caring. The only thing we can do now is get payback on the bastards that did it. And to do that, we need to stay alive."

"Understood. This is your domain, Jake. You're in charge. Get us out of here."

"Marcus, see what's out front."

Gray disappeared towards the front of the building while Hawk moved to the rear door to check outside. There were numerous figures coming their way, of which he counted maybe six or seven. He brought up the AK-12 and opened fire.

The trailing shooters scattered as bullets found a target and one of them dropped. They returned fire, bullets hammering into the door jamb.

Hawk ducked back, dropped out a magazine for a tactical reload, and rammed home a fresh one.

Gray reappeared, saying, "The street is clear out front. There are a few cars parked about, so there is some cover. But mostly it's open. That helicopter finds us, Jake, we're going to be in all sorts of pain."

Hawk nodded knowingly. "There's only one thing for it. We go underground. Do you have a light?"

"Yes. You?"

"Copy that. Find me a hole, Marcus."

"On it."

Fearing that something wasn't right, Hawk had gone into the operation decked out in full battle kit. This included fragmentation grenades, and as he pulled one from his webbing, he hurried again towards the back door.

This time seeing that the shooters were now much

closer, Hawk pulled the pin on the grenade and threw it along the street. "Frag out!"

The explosion rocked the alley. A ball of flame and smoke blew skyward like a volcanic eruption. As the echo died down, he could hear the cries of agony from some of their downed attackers.

Hawk opened fire, just enough to suppress the remaining operators from Noskov. He said into his comms, "Marcus, I need something, mate."

"Almost there, Jake. Give me a moment." There was a long pause before Gray's voice came back. "I've got us a way out."

"Roger that, coming to you."

Hawk moved back through the building and ran into Anja at the front near the main door. "Come on, boss, we've got to go."

She followed him out onto the street and keeping low, using the vehicles for cover, they moved towards where Gray waited for them.

"Down here."

Hawk wrinkled his nose. "Bloody hell. Smells like half of London shit down this hole."

"It's all we've got."

"After you."

One by one, they climbed down into the sewer, the overpowering smell almost making them retch. "Where to from here?" Gray asked.

"I would say follow your nose. But that might lead us up Shit Creek."

"Very funny, Jake, very funny."

———

IT TOOK them the best part of three hours to travel the next four blocks. Once they'd found an exit, they moved upward and emerged onto another street. Both men crouched around the hole, while Anja climbed out.

"You two stink," she said solemnly.

"I think it's Marcus, boss. I could swear he shit himself."

"Shut up, will you?" Gray growled. This was their way of dealing with loss.

Hawk said, "Could you imagine Karl down in that sewer?"

"He'd be bathing in hand sanitizer about now."

"If he was alive," said Anja looking down at her disheveled state to cover the grief she was feeling.

"Yeah. Let's find us some wheels."

———

"YOU SET US UP," Hawk hissed at Moreau. "Somehow you got wind of what was going to happen, and you hung us to dry out there. And now one of us is dead."

The Interpol agent winced. "I'm sorry. We weren't sure on our intel. I can honestly say we had no idea that it was going to be Noskov's men. We thought for sure it was going to be Boyle."

"That's bullshit, and you know it."

"Watch your mouth," snarled Fontaine.

"Don't you start, asshole. You're just as much to blame as what she is."

"Jake, this is not helping," Anja said calmly.

"It's bloody well helping me. You can't tell me they didn't know that Noskov's men were going to be there. We were put in play in the hope that that bastard was going to be there, too. What I can't work out is who authorized it."

"What do you mean?" Anja asked.

"Someone from the head shed gave them the green light to use us."

"Really?"

"Have you been able to get in touch with the secure facility yet?"

Anja shook her head. "No."

Hawk looked at Moreau. "I bet it's been shut down and Interpol has our pigeon. Isn't that right?"

The Interpol officer suddenly looked uncomfortable.

"And there you have your answer," Hawk continued. "Who was it?"

"It came from Hereford," Moreau conceded.

"The rotten bastards," Hawk growled. "They've got the biggest bus they could find and thrown us the fuck under it."

"Take it easy, Jake," said Anja. "I'll reach out and see if I can get an answer."

"I have a better idea. Get us on a plane and let's get back there. Ask the bastards face to face."

"All right, we'll do that."

Gray leaned over and whispered something in Hawk's ear. The former SAS man nodded, then once more turned his attention on Moreau. "Now you've got a job. You get the body of our mate back. Then you have it shipped home to Hereford."

"I'm not sure I can do that."

"You'll do it, all right. This is your shit. Clean it up."

"I'll see what I can do."

"Damn right you will."

———

Hereford, England

Hawk had been holding it in this whole time, waiting to hit someone. It turned out that Peacock was his man. The resounding crack echoed through the room, the impact of the fist on face vibrating up Hawk's arm into his shoulder.

"Jacob!" Anja exclaimed.

Standing off to one side was Ilse, looking better with each day that passed. Hawk shook his hand and stared down at the Global boss, now sitting on the tiled floor, a trickle of blood leaking from the corner of his mouth. "You got our man killed, bastard. You had that coming."

Peacock wiped at the corner of his mouth with the back of his hand. He nodded. "I expected that. But even if I had known, it wouldn't have changed my decision."

"The Talon operation is autonomous. Anja is our boss. She makes the decisions. She lives with the choices she makes. It's not for you lot to come along. It fucks everything up. Which you have been doing since we've started."

Peacock climbed to his feet. "You seem to have forgotten, Jake. It is my money that allows your operation to be autonomous."

"Guess what? We don't need your money anymore. We have our own."

The Global owner looked confused.

"That's right. We have our own little account. Right now, it tops out at just under four hundred million."

The man was stunned. "Where did you get all that from?"

"Proceeds of crime."

Peacock looked over at Anja. "Is this true?"

She nodded. "I had Karl put a little away for a rainy day. Right at this point, we're more autonomous than we've ever been before. It's up to you what happens next. Stop interfering and let us do our job. If you want oversight, leave it with Mary Thurston. We will operate under our own budget and acquire our own equipment and personnel. We will cap our finance at five-hundred million. Anything over that will go into Global accounts. And get our asset back from Interpol. He knows more about this network than anybody else. We haven't finished with him, yet. Not by a long shot."

"I suppose you want Grizz and his team back as well?"

Hawk nodded. "That goes without saying."

"No," Anja replied.

Those in the room stared at her. Hawk was confused. "Boss, what?"

"I think the more streamlined we are the better we will be able to operate," she explained. "Two field agents, one person in command, a computer tech, and an operations coordinator."

"All right," Peacock agreed. "We'll do it your way. Would you like personnel to find you a new tech?"

"No, we will do that. But if you can make sure Karl's body gets home OK."

"I will see to it. What are your plans? Am I allowed to ask?"

"We're going after Noskov."

"He's a hard man to find."

"We have an idea where he is. Karl found him before he died."

"Well, good luck."

———

"HOW DID HE TAKE IT?" Thurston asked.

"About as well as can be expected," Anja replied. "Are those files for me?"

She pushed them across the table. "They are. I ran down the list of names you gave me and collected all I could on them. Is there anyone in particular you're looking at?"

"Not me," Anja replied. She passed the files over to Ilse.

Thurston said, "There are seven files there. I know you asked for eight, but one of them sadly has died."

"I'm sure we can find someone here," Ilse said.

"If it helps, there were a couple of recommendations there from Slick. I marked them."

Slick was Sam Swift, the number one computer tech working with Team Reaper. Some said he was the best at what he did.

"Thank you."

"How are you doing, Ilse?" Thurston asked.

"Getting stronger every day. Not quite up to it yet but it won't be long."

Anja patted her hand. "Take your time. We're not going after Noskov without you."

"What about the Island?"

"It's under surveillance," Thurston explained. "At the moment there seems to be nothing out of the ordinary. However, if he's there, we'll find him."

"It's our only lead."

"I'm aware of that."

"I urge you not to wait on me." Ilse's tone was almost pleading.

"When the time is right, we'll move. Not before. Until then, find us another tech. Use Jake if you have to. At least it'll keep him busy and out of the pub."

———

Hereford, England

Ilse found Hawk at the Farmers Arms pub. He was there with Gray, swapping war stories from a bygone era. They were sitting in a corner by the fire, a great place to be, considering how cold and windy it was outside. Even the rain had begun a steady fall just before she stepped inside.

The smell of woodsmoke pleased her immensely. Under her arms, she had the folders. Approaching the two men, she smiled then found a spare seat and sat down, placing her load on the table.

Hawk looked across at her. This was the first time he'd actually been face to face with her since he'd returned from the mission. He knew what he wanted to say, but instead blurted, "They let you out, did they?"

"They gave me a job. They said I could use you if I wanted to. But first you need to buy me a beer."

"Anything for my lady?"

"Oh dear, now I'm royalty."

"Yeah, sorry. Figure of speech."

While Hawk went up to the bar, she passed a folder across to Gray. "You can help, too, Marcus."

The former para took the folder and opened it, but kept his eyes on Ilse. "What exactly am I helping with?"

"We need to replace Karl," she said quietly.

"Oh, I see."

When Hawk rejoined them, they already had the folders spread across the table. He looked down at them and said, "Are you sure we should be doing this here?"

"Beer will soften the blow," Ilse said.

For the next hour and a half, they worked through the names and pictures until they had it narrowed down to one.

Hawk looked at the picture. "Are we sure?"

"Yes," Ilse said.

"Marcus?"

"Yes."

"All right, it's back to you, Ilse."

"I'll reach out to Interpol and get her released."

Hawk shook his head. "The boss is really going to love this one."

————

ANJA STARED AT THE PICTURE. "Am I going to regret this?"

"It's possible. But we feel she is the best candidate for the position."

The person they were talking about was Slania

Albring. She was former Special Forces Group out of Belgium. But after three years there, had been plucked to go into intelligence. She was trained and very qualified for the job at hand. However, she was currently being held by Interpol on various warrants.

Anja glanced at the picture again. Slania had long dark hair and a narrow face. Her build was slim, but what really caught the Talon commander's attention was the tattoos which covered a good portion of her body. "She looks like the roof of the Sistine Chapel."

"Wasn't it you who taught us that looks can be deceiving?" Ilse asked.

"Alright. Go and talk to her. If she passes and she wants the job, hire her."

Ilse raised her eyebrows. "You want me to go?"

"Yes. Will that be a problem?"

"No, ma'am."

"Fine, arrange a flight. Take Jake with you."

Ilse hesitated. "Are you sure—"

"Is there a problem?"

"No. At least I don't think so."

"Then go. Get out of my sight. I don't want to see you for a couple of days. I'll call you back if I need to."

"Yes, boss."

Ilse scooped up the papers and photo from Anja's desk and put them back in the folder. "I'll see you when I get back," she called over her shoulder as she left the room.

CHAPTER SEVENTEEN

Lyon, France

THEY MET Slania in a Lyon cafe not far from the Rhone River. In her early thirties, she was naturally suspicious of the people who had just sprung her from prison and were now offering her work. Well-paid work at that.

"Who are you again?" she asked in an accented voice.

"We work for the Global Corporation," Ilse said. "We are a special task force set up to combat the sex trafficking market across the globe."

"You realize I have a job, right?" Slania inquired.

"Not anymore," Ilse replied. "Belgian intelligence has now disavowed you. Something about going rogue on an operation which led Interpol to lock you up."

"The prick deserved it."

Ilse nodded. "Even so, punching a French minister in the face isn't the smartest way to go about things."

Slania looked across at Hawk. "Am I going to have any trouble with you?"

Her jaw was set firm and her gaze rock hard, as though she was trying to stare Hawk down. He waited before answering, letting her know that he could not be intimidated. "Only if you fuck up."

"What do you need me for?"

"Your computer skills mainly," Ilse said. "Every now and again you might get shot at. So your military skills will come in handy as well."

"What happened to the last person?"

"He's dead," Hawk replied. "Do you want the job or not?"

"Maybe? But you seem to forget—" she held up her hands where the handcuffs were, "someone already has a prior claim."

"I wouldn't worry about that. Interpol owes us a favor or two."

"Then I will work for you. But I have terms, too."

"Oh, aye? This should be good."

"I don't do touching. You touch me, I'll break your hand. Do it a second time and I'll break your neck. Unless I initiate it. No one touches my stuff. Anything I bring with me is mine. I don't share."

"Anything else?"

"You don't question my decisions. If we are in the middle of an operation and I say to do something I expect it done. I gather that's what you want me for, to act as overwatch on operations?"

"If you can play nice with the team, then we might be able to work something out," Ilse said.

"I guess that is settled then."

Hawk stared at her. "The boss is going to love you."

"Really?"

"Yes. If she doesn't shoot you first."

———

Anja was in the gym working on her Shotokan Karate when Slania entered. Both women were wearing tank tops and sports leggings. Slania watched Anja work before moving over to commence her own workout.

The Talon commander watched as the newcomer began going through her paces. With the private jet arriving late the night before, the two hadn't been formally introduced yet. Anja lifted that way just to watch from afar. Then she continued with her own workout.

Before long, both women were dripping in sweat from their exertions. Anja took a break and toweled herself off. It wasn't long before Slania stopped to do the same.

Anja picked up a dry towel from the rack, then tossed it across to her. "You're not too bad at that."

"You, too. Do you work out much?"

"When I can."

Slania indicated some mats over near the wall for people to work out on. "Would you like to try a little friendly competition?"

Anja thought about it for a moment, then nodded. "Sure, why not?"

The pair walked across to the mats and dropped their towels to the side. Anja bent down to pick up a helmet sitting on a table. Slania said with a wry smile, "Are you sure we will need those?"

"Can't be too careful."

Minutes later, they were ready to go. Both wore helmets and Mixed Martial Arts gloves. They circled each other for a few seconds before Slania moved in with lightning speed. Her first punch missed, but her second caught Anja in the shoulder. Anja, however, moved with the punch and then dropped. She did the splits and then as Slania hovered above her, she came up with a counterpunch, driving just under the newcomer's solar plexus.

Anja heard the air rush from Slania's lungs. There was an audible grunt and then the newest member of the team stepped back, hunched over.

Moving like silk, Anja came to her feet and stepped back, started circling her opponent. Slania's head shot up, anger in her eyes.

From across the room, Hawk called out., having just entered with Ilse and Gray. The greeting was harmless, but the effect it had on Anja was catastrophic. She turned her head automatically to see what Hawk was doing, and Slania took the advantage.

She spun on her heel. Her right leg came up, driving power through her hips. Her foot caught Anja up beside her cheek, luckily on the padding of the helmet. Otherwise, the outcome could have been different.

From across the room, Hawk saw all, as Anja tumbled down onto all fours. He winced, as though he'd been the one impacted by the hit. "Ouch. I bet that hurt," he said to Ilse.

By the time they reached the mat, Anja was back on her feet, shaking her head to clear the cobwebs.

Slania had no intention of letting Anja regain her composure, as things started to heat up and get serious. She moved in close to swing a right at Anja's head, but the Talon commander was expecting it and moved accordingly. She blocked the blow, came in under the extended arm, and hit Slania a solid blow into her rib cage. Not once, but twice, causing the new Talon member to stagger.

Slania gasped, then moaned as she sank to her knees. Anja stood up and stood watching to see if the newcomer was all right.

Another ruse. Slania swept Anja's legs from beneath her, rolled onto her back, and brought her heel down onto the Talon commander's middle, driving the air from her lungs.

Hawk winced again as he felt the blow. "Bloody hell, I can't watch. It'll be a bloodbath."

"Really?" Ilse said. "I'll bet you fifty British Pounds that the boss kicks her ass."

"All right, you're on. Marcus, you want some of this action?"

"All right. I'm on the boss, I've seen her practicing her karate and I've come to the conclusion that she'd kick your scrawny ass, Jake."

Anja rolled over, coming to her hands and knees still taking in great lungfuls of air. Slania stood over her and said, "Have you had enough yet?"

Anja rocked back onto her knees. She looked up at Slania and shook her head. "Just catching my breath."

She stood up and started circling to her right this time. Slania followed her, feinting left and right as she went. For the next couple of minutes, the order of the day was thrust and parry. Then, thinking she saw an opening, Slania moved in for a wicked blow to Anja's ribs.

However, Anja was waiting. She twisted her body at the hips. The blow skidded across her ribs before she brought her hand down, chopping across the back of Slania's exposed neck.

The new Talon member staggered and went down to one knee. Anja moved in close and brought her own knee up to the side of Slania's head. The blow could have been shattering if she hadn't held back. But it was devastating enough to almost knock her out.

Slania rolled over onto her back, eyes seemingly whirling in her head. She laid there panting hard before Anja moved in close, standing over her. "Have *you* had enough?"

The Belgian nodded slowly. "I think maybe yes."

Anja held out her hand to lift her up off the mat. Slania took it and the Talon commander pulled her up.

"Welcome to Talon. My name is Anja Meyer. I'm in charge."

"No shit?"

"You call me ma'am or boss."

Ilse held out her hand. "You owe me fifty pounds."

"So much for the no touching rule."

Slania looked at Hawk. She winked at him, giving him a wry grin. "The bloody cow was having a lend of me."

Anja took off her gloves. "If we're all finished here, we've got work to do. Everybody in the operations room in thirty minutes. We have a visitor."

———

UNDER THE WATCHFUL supervision of an armed guard, Leonid Fedorov was waiting for them. When they entered the room, he looked up and smiled at Anja. "Ah, my favorite person."

"And not mine," she shot back at him. "Everybody, take a seat."

Once they had all settled, Anja started talking. "Slania, welcome to Task Force Talon. You've met everyone I think except for Marcus."

The Belgian looked across the table at the former Para. She nodded her head. "I am Slania Albring."

"Marcus Gray. Pleased to meet you."

"Our friend over here," said Anja, "is Leonid Fedorov. He is scum, but he is helpful."

He gave her a hurt look. "I am offended."

"Be thankful you're here at Hereford and not in a deep hole somewhere."

"Which begs the question, why am I here?"

"We've had people watching Tagomago Island, and there is no sign of Noskov," Anja explained. "So, where is he?"

Fedorov stabbed a finger in her direction. "You know,

this is what I like about you. You are never one to be short of a difficult question. My answer to you is, I have no bloody idea."

"Then you better start thinking, or you will find your way back to that deep dark hole."

"Is there anyone there at all?"

"A few people, not many."

"Then Noskov will be there."

Anja stared at his face, he seemed adamant. "What makes you so certain, if we have not laid eyes on him yet?"

"Just because you haven't seen him doesn't mean he is not there."

"Explain, blast you," Hawk demanded. "Stop playing these bloody games. Keep it up and I'll let the new girl come over there and smack you in the mouth."

Federov grinned. "I'm not sure that would be such a bad thing. If I was not engaged with a previous offer, I would even consider taking the young lady out for lunch."

"Fuck off, Fedorov. Just answer the question."

"Where shall I start? Back in the early days of World War Two, the Nazis built a U boat base under the island. It was actually quite a marvelous engineering feat. When Viktor was still alive, he would often go there. He had it converted into something like an underground mansion."

"It still doesn't mean he will be there."

"He will be there."

Gray leaned forward. "How impenetrable is it?"

Federov grinned again. "No, it will be hard, but there are ways."

"What ways?" Hawk asked him.

"There is an air conditioning vent coming out of the side of the cliff. There would be some climbing involved, but it is big enough to allow a man to pass through it."

"Can you show us where it is?"

The Russian shrugged. "Do you have a map?"

Hawk pushed a laptop towards Slania. "It is time to earn your money."

She opened the laptop and began typing. Moments later, she had a map of the island sitting before her on the screen. She looked over at Fedorov and said, "If you think I'm coming over there for you to look at this, think again. Get off your ass."

"Let me help," said Hawk.

The former SAS operator got off his seat, then grabbed Fedorov by the shirt collar. He dragged him to his feet and then around to the other side of the table so he could stand behind Slania and see the screen. "Show her."

Fedorov leaned in and stabbed at the screen with his finger. "It should be about there."

"What if it's blocked? Is there any other way of getting in?"

The Russian turned and looked at Hawk. There was a spark in his eye as he said, "You could always walk in the front door."

"Shut up and sit back down." Hawk stared at the screen. Then he said to Slania, "Gather us all the Intel you can. Whatever it takes."

"If I could find a blueprint of the complex, that would really help us."

Ilse looked at Fedorov. "If Viktor converted it, then there would be one there somewhere. Where did he keep it, Leonid?"

"Where he kept everything valuable. An online safe."

"A what?" Hawk asked.

"An online safe. An electronic safe. It's like having a safe online where you can keep all your valuable documents and things like that. It is run by the Bank of Switzerland."

"So all we have to do is break into it?" Slania asked.

"That is about it. But don't expect it to be as easy as

what you think. There are three or four safeguards just to get into it. That's without getting into the bank's system."

Slania grinned. It was the first one Hawk had seen from her and it changed her normally hard face to a very attractive one. "I do love a good challenge."

Anja looked at Federov. "What else did he keep in there?"

"Different documents. A list of his customers. Any dirty secrets he might need to hold against certain people. Things they didn't want getting out."

Turning to face Slania, Anja said, "I've heard of these things, but I've never come across one. Have you?"

"A couple of times. I won't say it's easy, but it's not impenetrable. The main problem will be getting through the bank's security system. Most of them these days, if an alarm is triggered it is usually silent and what happens is that a worm comes out and piggybacks its way to the host computer. If that happens, we're in trouble."

"I have a question," asked Hawk. "Will it still be active even after he's dead?"

"They are a lifetime thing. The only access into them is if it's been left to you in a will. If there are no next of kin, no one gets into it."

"Then I guess we have work to do."

The meeting broke up and Ilse pulled Hawk aside. "What are you going to need for the operation?"

"Scuba gear, wet suits. Maybe some climbing equipment. I think we'll go in with suppressed MP5s."

"What about explosives? Grenades? Anything like that?"

"Maybe some breaching charges? Grenades, definitely. Somehow, I think we might need a boat."

Ilse nodded. "Will a RHIB do?"

"Couldn't ask for anything better," Hawk replied.

She stared at him for a long moment. He cocked an eyebrow. "What?"

"We haven't had much time together since you've been back."

"Yeah. We'll have to find some."

"Do you still want to go ahead with it, Jake?"

"Yes. We've just got to work out how we're going to do it."

Ilse leaned in and kissed his cheek.

Hawk raised his hand and placed it on her shoulder. His finger extended and rubbed against the exposed flesh on her neck. "Once this whole Medusa thing is over and Noskov is gone, we'll sit down and we'll map this whole thing out."

"I'll hold you to that."

"I expect you to. Now, you're going to need weapons as well. You'd better fit yourself with one of those bullet-proof suits, too."

Ilse frowned. "Why?"

"Because we're going to need someone to drive our boat. You're it. You can do that, can't you?"

"Better than you drive cars. Speaking of which."

"I drive just fine," he replied with a wicked grin.

"Don't tell the boss that, she'll fall over backwards."

"Don't tell her what?" Anja asked.

"That Jake thinks he's a good driver."

"Good grief," she said, rolling her eyes. "The only place he would be a good driver is in a taxi in India."

Hawk gave her a playful, offended look. "I'm not that bad, boss."

"Tell that to the cars you've written off recently."

"Not my fault."

Anja said, "If Slania is successful in getting the blue-prints for the island, you'll need a plan on my desk within a day. Failing that, then we're going to have to do the recon ourselves. And if we get caught, it'll just blow everything out of the water."

"Let's hope she comes through then."

"Yes, let's."

———

"BASTARD," Slania hissed as she banged her hand on the desk beside the computer keyboard. "How many more times?"

Hawk said, "What's up?"

"Someone on the other end keeps trying to ping me."

"Ping you?"

"Yes. I'm using a new ghost program that Belgian intelligence was running just before I got farcically locked up. They know I'm there, but they can't find me. And if they can't find me, they can't shut the system down. However, it doesn't mean they can't keep looking."

"And?"

"And because I keep doing it, it's as slow as shit."

"How much have you got left to do?"

"I just have to breach one more safeguard." Slania wrote numbers on the pad beside her.

"What are you doing there?" Hawk asked.

"I'm writing out code so I can get back in. Every time I pull out it all locks behind me. So then I have to go back through it. If I write down the code, it's just quicker."

"What happens if they catch you?"

"They engage a lock which shuts everything down. Then within two days all the coding is changed out, and I have to start again. It can turn a couple of day job into a couple of weeks. Is there any news regarding the operation?"

Hawk shook his head. "Still no sign. All we can do is take Fedorov's word for it."

"Who is that guy, anyway?"

"That guy was Viktor Medvedev's right-hand man. We've had him locked away all safe and sound and he's been helping us out with a few things. He is an actual font of information."

"Do you trust him?"

Hawk snorted. "About as far as I can kick the bludger. He tried a few games with us early on, but since then we've sort of knocked him into line."

While she typed, Slania said to Hawk, "Can I ask you a question?"

"Go for it."

"How did you all come to be working for this—whatever it is?"

"The boss used to work with German intelligence. Same with Ilse. They had an op go south when the shit hit the fan. The boss's masters blamed it all on her and she was forced out. I was former SAS working with MI6. An op went to crap. Anja found me in the bottom of a bottle. Marcus is former Para, not a bad bloke either. He doesn't have all the shit that we came with. We were all top tier operators nobody wanted. I'll tell you this though, we're all bloody good at what we do. Even the ones who aren't with us anymore."

Hawk looked up and saw Ilse coming towards them. "How are things going?"

Slania said, "I should be able to crack it today, providing that this guy on the other end gives me a break."

"Any news?" Hawk asked her.

"Still no sign."

"Then the assumption is still the same."

"Yes, it is."

———

"THERE." Slania slapped an A4 sheet of paper on the table in front of Anja. "We're in."

The Talon commander picked it up and looked it over. "Good work."

"There was also something else."

Anja looked up with an inquisitive frown. "Something else, what?"

Slania held out a second piece of paper. Anja took it and scanned the writing. "Are we sure about this?"

"It came from within, so, yes, I would say that it checks out."

"This is all I need." Anja picked up her phone and selected a contact then pressed the green call button. She tapped the table while waiting for the connection to go through. When it was answered on the other end, she said, "I need you now."

When she disconnected, she looked up at Slania and said, "Find me Jake. Tell him to bring his personal weapon. You, too."

"Yes, boss."

————

"WHAT IS THIS?" Peacock asked as he looked up from his work to stare at the four people standing before him. "It looks like a blasted mutiny."

Hank Jones tossed the paper in his calloused hand onto the desk. "Why don't you tell us, George."

The Global CEO looked confused. He picked up the paper and with each word his face became noticeably paler. Anja said, "I was hoping that this wasn't right, but it is, isn't it?"

Peacock kept reading.

"It would explain a lot of things, George," Jones said in his deep voice.

"Like cutting Grizz from our team," Hawk said. "Medusa suddenly appearing in our AO. Was it you who leaked about Hermann?"

"I—I don't know what you're talking about."

"It's right there in front of you," Jones said.

"Medvedev was paying you for work. You had black teams in the Medusa fold. Shit, Boyle and his men are one of them."

"You don't understand."

"Don't bother trying to justify this. MI6 are sending men to pick you up. You can explain it all to them."

Peacock's hand darted to the phone on his desk. Anja said, "Don't bother. All communications out of the building have been cut until we're done here."

But the Global CEO wasn't done yet. The same hand moved for the top drawer where he kept a Glock.

Hawk shot him in the shoulder. It probably wasn't necessary, but it made the Talon agent feel better. Peacock grunted in pain, sweat breaking out on his brow.

Hawk stepped forward and said, "Did you warn Noskov we were onto him?"

"I have nothing to say."

Hawk hit him.

"Jake," Anja cautioned him.

"Stab him in the eye with his pen," Slania said.

"Not helping," Anja replied to her comment.

Jones nodded. "I like this girl. She has good ideas."

"You mean she's not British," Hawk shot back at him.

"She's not you."

Hawk ignored the barb and moved closer to Peacock. "I never thought you'd be one to turn on your own. Now, answer the question or I might just stab you in the eye with the pen. And you know me, it's not often I don't follow through on what I say I'm going to do."

Peacock nodded. "Yes."

"Bollocks. Where is he?"

"He left."

"I already figured that out. Where was he going?"

"He has a place—or rather Medvedev had a place."

"Where?"

"The Tabernas Desert."

"Spain?"

Peacock nodded. "Yes."

"Where?"

"I don't know."

Hawk's Glock came up. Anja stepped forward. "Wait, Jacob. Leonid will know."

Satisfied, Hawk shot him.

Anja glared at him. "What was that?"

"He was responsible for Karl being killed. He got what he deserved." Hawk looked at Jones. "You got any objections?"

The former general shook his head. "For once we agree on something."

Hawk looked at Anja who still wasn't happy. "If you want to be part of this team, you will follow orders. Understood?"

"Yes, ma'am."

"Now we need to talk to Federov and find out where Noskov is."

Indicating with his hand, Jones said, "I'll take care of this."

"What happens now?" Anja asked the big man.

"There will be a meeting with the board, but until then I will take over until it can be sorted. I'll let Mary know what is happening; she's out with Team Reaper on a mission. Good luck, Miss Meyer. And well done."

"Thank you, sir."

———

FEDEROV GREETED them with his customary smile. "You just caught me. I was about to board my flight to places unknown."

Anja stared at him. "Tabernas Desert."

"Spain, yes."

"Where did Medvedev have his base?"

"Why would you want to know that?" Federov asked.

"Where?" Hawk snapped, growing impatient.

"The Zamora Ammunition Factory," Federov replied.

Hawk gave him a skeptical look. "An ammunition factory in the desert?"

"Yes, it was built in the fifties. Abandoned three years later. Viktor started using it five years ago. It is a complex set inside of a cliff."

"More than one way in?" Hawk asked.

"Yes. There are three. Four if you count the escape tunnel."

"You need to show Slania where all the entrances are."

"All right."

"Good, get it done. We're wasting time."

CHAPTER EIGHTEEN

Tabernas Desert, Spain

THE DESERT NIGHT WAS COLD. Almost bitterly so. Hawk and Gray set the final charges at the mouth of the escape tunnel and then dragged the guard back inside. Overhead in a Boeing C-17 Globemaster III was the rest of the team. The aircraft had been supplied as an airborne command post where Anja, Ilse, and Slania were set up at their consoles.

It hadn't come cheap. To set up the operation, twenty million dollars had been pulled from their newly acquired budget and been paid to Global. The price of operating autonomously.

Hawk said into his comms. "Alpha, this is Bravo One. The charges are in place, moving to primary insertion point."

"Bravo One from Alpha One, copy, moving to primary insertion point."

The two operators hurried to their DPV (Desert Patrol Vehicle) which had been dropped at the same time they were. It looked like an armed dune buggy, but it had grunt and firepower.

Climbing in they drove the circuitous one-kilometer route to where they would leave it and begin their assault on foot.

Both wore their Synoprathetic suits beneath their clothing, now learning firsthand that the suits used their body heat to keep them warm even on nights like this one. Both were armed with Heckler & Koch 416s, suppressed. They carried fragmentation grenades and stun grenades too. Additionally, they had ballistic helmets with NVGs attached. They went in heavy with ammunition, in case the extra firepower was required.

Hawk pulled in behind a low, scarred ridge and then alighted from the vehicle. They climbed the ridge and lay belly down to prevent skylining themselves to the two guards below them. "Alpha One, Bravo Team is in position."

"Roger, Bravo One."

"Alpha Three, sitrep?"

"Still only two X-Rays, Bravo One. External power source is two hundred meters to your left."

"Copy, I can hear."

"Bravo One, from Alpha Two, copy?"

"Roger, send traffic."

Ilse said, "Final update. As you know, we've had ISR circulating throughout the day, and we're still unclear of how many X-Rays are onsite. Estimate at least ten. Your call."

"Roger, Alpha Two. Commencing insert. Out."

"Copy, good luck."

"Ready to kick these pricks in the bollocks, Marcus?" Hawk asked.

"Let's do it."

"We take the X-Rays first and then cut the power. Once that's done, we blow the exits."

"On your six, Jake."

They came down off the ridge, moving with stealth.

At the base they took up positions behind some old 44-gallon drums and prepared to fire at the two guards at the entrance.

"Ready?" Hawk asked.

"Just say when."

"Three...two...one...execute."

Both suppressed 416s spat their deadly rounds at the two guards. The men jerked and they went down. "Check them, Marcus while I take out the power."

"Copy."

Hawk hurried across to where the large generator sat pumping power into the underground complex. Once he reached it, he squatted down beside the big diesel, taking out the explosives, and affixing them to the machine.

Moments later, the explosives were ready to detonate. He set the timer for two minutes and then hurried across to where Gray waited for him. "We're set to go."

"As soon as it goes off, I'll remote detonate," Gray replied.

The timing of the explosion seemed to take hours instead of what remained of the two minutes. Hawk was becoming impatient, but moments later it detonated.

An orange fireball reached into the clear sky, rolling up like a mushroom. The sound of the explosion rolled across the desert, buffeting the surrounding ridges.

Beside Hawk, Gray said, "Firing."

The two men felt rather than saw or heard the other three explosions which seem to be swallowed by the surrounding landscape. Hawk said into his comms, "Alpha, we're breaching now."

"Good luck, Bravo. Godspeed."

The mine entrance to the tunnel was as wide as a dual lane highway. Hawk guessed that the width was to allow easy access for trucks coming to the complex to collect the ammunition as it was manufactured.

They hugged the wall to the left as the road inside

curved in that direction. Already they could hear cries of alarm from deep within the cliff. The sides of the tunnel were made of concrete and in places, even through the green haze of the NVGs, they looked to have been reinforced.

Suddenly, up ahead, two figures appeared. Hawk stroked the trigger on his 416 and the first one went down in a tangle of arms and legs. Gray took care of the second one as he repeated the dose of violence that Hawk had just executed.

The two Talon men remained silent as they pressed forward. As they stepped over the two fallen X-Rays, they placed a round each into the corpses to ensure they stayed down.

Thirty meters further along, the wall to their right opened up into a large, cavernous room. Hawk swept it as he went past and guessed that one time in its life, it had been a large storage area. They continued their sweep forward.

"Alpha, this is Bravo, comms check, over."

"Still read you five by five, Bravo."

"Roger that."

Another figure appeared ahead of them, and without breaking stride, Hawk fired again. This time three rounds and the figure went down without a sound. The sound of spent casings tinkled on the concrete floor.

After passing two more storage rooms, Hawk figured they'd gone maybe 150 meters before the complex really opened out in front of them. "Sweet mother of God."

"I bet you never expected something like that," whispered Gray.

"It's fucking huge."

Before them, an enormous cavern had been hollowed out inside the cliff. Inside that cavern were at least four large warehouses, and other buildings. It was easy to make out, even with the NVGs on.

Hawk guessed that the inside looked pretty much like it had done way back when it was first established. Flashlight beams danced around everywhere ahead of them as people tried to work out what was going on. Somewhere off to the right, the two Talon operators heard someone shouting about the exit tunnel being caved in.

Already, panic was starting to filter amongst the occupants.

A figure appeared with a flashlight and Gray opened fire. The man fell, crying out in pain. "Where the hell are we meant to find him in this place?"

Hawk took cover behind a 44-gallon drum. "Let's just kill them all, and hope we get lucky."

Gunfire erupted to their front and bullets cracked overhead. Gray grunted. "Looks like someone has NVGs."

"Now the fun really begins, Mucker."

They returned fire and then moved while the shooter was behind cover. With their weapons still raised, they pressed forward, towards the threat. Then as soon as he reappeared, they fired once more, neutralizing the threat without further ado.

Beside Gray, Hawk said with determination, "Let's go to war."

———

ILYA NOSKOV WAS CONCERNED. Somehow, he'd been found, and now, whoever it was had mounted a full-scale assault. "Get the power back up," he snarled at one of his men. A flashlight sat on his desk and the glow it cast made him look like a monster from the depths of hell.

The man disappeared and Noskov turned to Boyle. "Do something." There was panic in the leader's voice. If this had been Medvedev, there would have been no such thing.

Boyle said, "They've blown all of the exits except for the main entrance."

"Then gather your men and secure it."

"They're working on it as we speak."

"We need a backup. Get the vehicles ready, we'll shoot our way out of here. Have the countdown sequence started."

"I'll see to it now."

"Do not fail me, Lester."

The man made it sound like everything that was happening was his fault. The truth was, Noskov was reckless. For years, Medusa had lived in the shadows; now it was out in the open and fractured badly. Noskov had lost his grip on everything thanks to the Talon team.

Splinter groups had now formed amongst the buyers and Noskov was in as much trouble from them as he was from the newly formed Talon and other law enforcement agencies.

"I suggest we get out, sir. Forget what you have here and fall back to a new secure facility."

"What if that is compromised as well?" the Russian demanded.

"Then we will find another."

"Fine, we'll do it your way. Get your men together."

"What about your men?" Boyle asked.

"Sacrifices must be made."

Though not you. "Be ready to go in five minutes, sir. I'll be back."

"Just hurry."

———

HAWK LET his 416 drop to his side, the strap catching it. As it fell, he brought up his Glock and put two rounds into the chest of a man in front of him. Then he swiveled at the hips and fired two more at another attacker to his right. A heartbeat later, the man joined his friend on the cold hard floor of the complex.

Suddenly Hawk heard the staticky squawk from a radio attached to the dead man's belt. "Cover me, Marcus."

He bent down and released the walkie talkie from the belt. He held it up and listened.

Team One and Two pull back to the vehicles. I say again, Team One and Team Two pull back to the vehicles. Team Three, clear us a path out of here.

They're getting out. And by the sounds of it, they thought they were under attack by more than two shooters.

"Marcus, they're going to make—" Bullets cut between them.

Gray opened fire and the shooting stopped. "What?"

"They're trying to make a break for it. We need to make sure that doesn't happen."

"You got any explosive left?"

"Some."

"I've got an idea."

———

BOYLE CLIMBED into the front armored SUV's passenger seat while the rest of his men piled into their assigned vehicles. Every man was ready to go, dressed in battle kit and armed to the eyeballs.

Boyle said into his comms. "Call in."

"Car One, ready," the driver beside him said.

"Two ready."

"Three ready."

"Four is ready."

Boyle nodded. "Let's roll."

The SUVs started moving, slowly at first but then they picked up speed. Headlights danced around in the darkness as they turned left and right to negotiate their way towards the main exit.

Once clear they would head south towards Almeria. The next leg was from there to the port and board a boat to Oran in Algeria. They would then escort Noskov to Libya to yet another supposed safe haven.

But first they had to get out of here.

Boyle looked down at the illuminated face of his watch. They had five minutes before the charges would bring the whole cavern down upon the complex.

"Keep moving," Boyle said into his comms. "Team Three, I need a sitrep."

"No joy," came the reply.

"Say again?"

"No joy, boss. We can't find them."

"Then get out before this place comes down."

The driver in Boyle's SUV swerved to the right; behind them, he saw in the side mirror, the others following like a snake.

Boyle knew they were close to the tunnel now; it was somewhere up ahead of them. The headlights on their vehicle illuminated the opening in front of them and the mercenary felt the SUV surge as the driver fed it some more gas.

Boyle looked again at his watch. Time was ticking down. He said into his comms, "Team Three, are you moving?"

"Copy, we're getting mobile now."

"Roger. We're approaching the exit. Catch us up when you—"

Suddenly the world exploded. Orange flames reached up while the blast wave thrust the SUV violently sideways like a giant hand.

The windows facing the blast disintegrated allowing

red hot flames to enter. The SUV hit the concrete wall throwing those within around like rag dolls.

Boyle lay stunned, blood running down one side of his face while the flesh on the other had already blistered and melted like butter.

Then came more explosions and the sound of gunfire.

CHAPTER NINETEEN

Tabernas Desert, Spain

"FRAG OUT!" Hawk shouted as he lobbed another grenade at the shooters sheltering around the rear vehicle. It exploded and sprayed the shooters with shrapnel.

The two Talon operators steadily worked their way through the mercenaries with shot and frag from the shadows. Men fell like tenpins into bloody heaps.

Suddenly the SUV which had been third in line swung out wide and sped forward, making a break for the tunnel. It avoided the one which had been knocked out in the blast, and sped away.

As Hawk reloaded, he said into his comms, "Alpha Three, copy?"

"Copy, Bravo." The voice was faint, staticky.

"There is an SUV breaking out. Watch it."

"Roger."

"Frag out!" Gray shouted.

The explosion rang out and more mercenaries died. As he scanned the scene before him, Hawk noticed movement in the lead SUV which had borne the brunt of the blast. He hurried across to it and looked inside, flicking on the small flashlight, seeing the battered and burned face of Boyle.

"Things get a bit warm for you?"

"Fuck you."

"Where's Noskov?'

"Third SUV."

Shit. "Guess we'll catch up to him. Where's he going?"

"A—Almeria."

"Fine, we'll find him there."

"Good luck. You stay here m—much longer you w—won't go anywhere," Boyle managed to get out.

"What do you mean?" Hawk demanded.

Gray appeared beside Hawk. "You want to do some shooting anytime soon?"

"Something's not right," Hawk replied as bullets punched into the SUV. He looked back at Boyle. "What do you mean, Lester?"

The dying man gave a half grin. "Boom."

"Christ. Marcus, we have to—"

The rumbling started at the rear of the cavern and started rolling towards them, growing into thunderous booms.

"Marcus, move!"

The two Talon operators started running towards the tunnel as the explosions steadily started to catch up with them.

"Run faster," Hawk yelled.

The booming grew louder, almost deafening and then it was upon them. First at the entrance to the cavern, then halfway along the entrance tunnel. Jolting explosions which brought the ceiling down.

———

"What just happened?" Anja asked anyone who was listening over their internal comms system aboard the C-17. It didn't matter who, just as long as someone answered her.

"I don't know," Ilse replied.

"Slania?"

"Wait one." She adjusted her settings for her ISR coverage and studied the screen.

The others stared at her, waiting for an answer. It was like they were hanging off every word Slania was saying, except she wasn't saying anything. Within moments they were quickly growing impatient and were about to press her further when she said, "Explosions. Big ones."

"How big?"

Slania hesitated and then said, "Big enough to bring the cliff down."

"Damn it," Anja growled. "Bravo, this is Alpha One, copy?"

Nothing.

"Bravo, this is Alpha One, do you copy?"

Nothing.

"Bravo, this is Alpha One. Break squelch if you can hear me, over."

Again nothing.

The three women glanced at each other, none wanting to voice what they were all thinking.

"Bravo One, this is Alpha Two, come in, Jake."

Static.

Ilse looked at Slania. "Is the uplink still operational?"

She checked and after a few moments, nodded. "Yes, it's fine. They're just not answering."

Ilse looked at Anja. "Ma'am."

The Talon commander read her mind. "Yes. Jack, can you hear me?"

A British voice came back. "Yes, I can hear you."

"Can you take us down to ten thousand feet. We've lost comms and are trying to reestablish them."

"Yes, ma'am, taking her down to ten thousand."

"Thank you."

The pitch of the C-17 engines changed immediately as the nose came down and the plane dropped altitude.

For the next few minutes, they tried to raise the two men on the ground. Still, they heard nothing.

"Ma'am, we're at ten thousand and holding," the pilot said over the radio.

"Thank you, Jack."

"Bravo One, this is Alpha One, do you copy?"

Nothing.

"Bravo, come in, over."

Static then, "Read you, Alpha, Bravo is a party of two and we're still in the fight."

Relief flooded through the three women and Anja said, "Good to hear your voice, Jake."

Tabernas Desert, Spain

The two Talon operators strode out of the tunnel covered in dust. Behind them the entrance had collapsed trapping those who were still alive inside.

"What now, Jake?" Gray asked.

"We go after that damn SUV. Noskov isn't getting away this time."

They hurried to where they'd left the DPV, climbed in, and started the motor. "Alpha Three, copy?"

"Read you Lima Charlie, Bravo."

"I need you to find me that SUV if you can. It's headed to Almeria."

"I'll start a sweep."

"What's so important with the SUV, Jake?" Anja asked, already knowing what the answer would be.

"Noskov bailed," Hawk replied as he started south through the desert. "Boyle said he was headed to Almeria. If he beats us there, it will be a bitch to find him."

"Copy. I'll have the plane divert there. We'll put down on the strip outside of town."

The strip she referred to was an old Spanish airbase which had been in use up until a few years before. Hopefully it would still be capable of taking a plane the size of the C-17.

Hawk looked to the east and saw the faint glow of dawn on the horizon. "Copy, ma'am."

"Keep me updated, Jake."

"We'll keep the updates coming. Just find me that SUV."

———

NOSKOV WAS RATTLED. They'd only just escaped the violent ambush and now they were hurtling through the desert towards Almeria.

All he had for protection were the three men with him, part of Boyle's mercenary team. He needed more. He picked up the satellite phone. Peacock would help him. After all, they were his men.

The phone on the other end rang.

"Hello?"

The voice was deep, not Peacock at all. "Who is this?"

"Who is this?" the voice shot back at him.

Noskov disconnected the call.

Instinctively he leaned closer to the window and looked up, wondering if anyone was watching.

"Is there a problem, sir?" the man in the front passenger seat asked him.

"I'm not sure. I think we could be being tracked."

"The vehicle was checked before we left," the man replied.

"No, I mean from above."

"We have contingencies for that, sir. Once we reach Almeria, we should be able to rectify the situation if it is so."

"Rectify? How?"

"Let us worry about that," the man replied.

Noskov looked out the window at the glow on the horizon. It would be full daylight soon, making it dangerous for him to be out in the open.

The Russian started to dial another number.

———

"ANY UPDATE ON THAT SUV, YET?" Hawk asked.

"Not yet," Slania replied. "I had to turn the UAV back so I'm trying to link up another satellite."

"Shit, he's going to get away, isn't he?"

"Not yet."

The sun had been up for two hours. Another hour of driving and they would be in Almeria. The road they followed was currently gravel but would join asphalt twenty kilometers further along.

"How are we off for fuel?" Hawk asked Gray.

"We should get there. Just."

"Hey, Bravo Team, I just picked up something interesting on ISR. I'm not sure what to make of it, but it can't be good."

"What do you have?"

"It looks like a Spanish Eurocopter Tigre," Slania said. "Coming in low."

"Crap, keep an eye on it. Marcus, looks like we've got inbound company. How's your defensive driving?"

"About as good as your golf."

"Then it should make for interesting reading." Hawk

checked the M240 machinegun in front of him. "Kick this thing in the guts, Marcus."

The DPV sped up and the dust cloud trailing it grew larger, hanging in the still desert air like a beacon.

"Bravo One, that helicopter has just changed course and is now headed straight at you."

"Copy, Alpha Three. You don't have a fast mover hidden away up there somewhere, do you?"

"Do ex-husbands count? Last time I saw him he was moving pretty fast."

"Child support?"

"Nine-millimeter."

"That'll do it."

"Helo is one mike out, Bravo. Just in case, good luck."

"We'll need every inch of it."

"Bravo, Alpha One."

"Copy, boss."

"The only ones in Spain who have these types of helicopters are military," Anja said. "I guess you know what that means?"

"Not shooting unless shot at. Same old ROEs," Hawk said, annoyed.

"We don't want some incident which will blow up into something—"

"Thirty seconds," Slania said.

"Love to chat longer, boss, but I'm about to get busy. Talk to you on the other side."

"Jake—"

BOOM!

The helicopter passed low overhead before banking and coming back around in a steep arc. Right away, Hawk knew it was going to attack and he readied himself for the coming onslaught.

Hawk stared at the flying weapon. He guessed it would be armed with Hydra 70 unguided rockets and possibly Spike Missiles. But it was the Giat 30mm cannon mounted in the chin turret which opened fire first.

Huge geysers of desert earth suddenly erupted skyward with each cannon round impact. Gray swung on the wheel of the DPV, and it began to slide sideways, so he gunned the motor to straighten it up.

Hawk opened fire with the M240 but by then it was too late and the Eurocopter had disappeared overhead.

"He won't do that again," Hawk said.

"Do what?" Gray shouted. "Shoot cannon shells at us? Next time it'll be fucking missiles."

"Or rockets," Hawk said.

"Or both."

"Jake, the chopper is coming back around. He's going to hit you from the west."

"Copy," Hawk replied. He pointed to the west. "Climb that ridge, now."

Gray never questioned the order, just turned the wheel, hard.

The DPV left the desert road and bounced through a shallow gully. Hawk gripped the LMG and waited for what he knew was coming. "Bravo Three, I need a sitrep on the helicopter."

"You should be seeing it in five...four...three...two...one."

When Slania had reached two, Hawk opened fire. The Eurocopter exploded over the ridge and into the spray of machinegun fire. Bullets peppered it as it passed over them and Hawk gave a grunt of appreciation. "That'll make him think twice."

The DPV launched over the crest of the low ridge and started down the other side. With it between them and the Eurocopter, they might stand a chance.

"Where is it, Alpha Three?"

"Circling around to the south. You should—shit. It's fired, break right!"

Gray spun the wheel and the DPV threatened to roll as it approached the point of no return. But it held and righted itself just as the missile impacted close by.

The two Talon operators felt the blast buffet the DPV and the warmth of the explosion. Hawk ground his teeth together as he braced himself. When everything seemed fine, he looked around the sky for the attacker.

It appeared seemingly out of nowhere and fired two rockets. Gray swung on the wheel again and the rockets missed and exploded beyond them.

"Are you going to shoot that thing down anytime soon?" Gray growled.

"I'd be fine if you could drive right."

"Typical SAS; can't shoot for shit. You should have joined the Paras."

Hawk said, "Alpha Three, talk to me. We can't keep this up."

"He's coming at you low from the west. He should crest that ridge in one mike."

"How low?" Gray asked.

"Ten meters."

Gray grinned and floored the gas pedal. "Ever seen that movie, Die Hard where Bruce Willis takes down that chopper?"

"What? Oh no, cock, don't try that bollocks with me. That's why it's called special effects."

The DPV started up the low ridge, still gaining speed. Gray said, "Get ready, Jake."

"Don't be a frigging loon, Marcus. You'll kill the both of us."

"Don't forget to put your head between your legs and kiss your ass goodbye."

"Bastard."

Still the DPV climbed gaining speed. Soon it was almost to the crest, a flat rock at the top looking like a readymade ramp.

"Come on, you bitch," Gray snarled trying to urge every last ounce of power from the machine.

They were about to hit when he shouted, "Now! Out!"

The pair flung themselves out of the DPV just as it lifted clear of the ridge. Pain shot through Hawk as he landed hard.

The vehicle traveled skyward, the motor screaming. Up and up and just as it reached the peak of its arc the helicopter appeared—

And missed it by a good twenty feet.

The DPV crashed down the other side of the ridge, rolling violently before exploding into flames.

Hawk came up onto his knees and looked across at Gray who was slowly dragging himself up. "Are you alright?" he asked the former para.

"I think so."

Hawk coughed. "Good, wait right there until I can come over and give you a right bollocking."

"Bravo, this is Alpha Two, sitrep, over."

"Copy Alpha Two. We're still in the fight. Even after Gray tried to kill us."

"Hang tough, help is on the way."

The helicopter came over once again, the cannon thundering this time. Dirt and rock kicked up all around them, showering them in debris. "Shit a brick," Hawk muttered.

Once more, the Eurocopter circled around, ready for another attack. The two Talon members hugged the ground as best they could, waiting for it to finish them off.

This time would be rockets. It had to be. It was more devastating that way. The thump of the rotors grew louder as it came in. Hawk and Gray slid down the slope of the ridge, trying to stay clear of the incoming attack.

Then suddenly the helicopter exploded in midair. With a loud roar, a jet fighter flew over them. Hawk looked up and saw a Lockheed Martin F-35B Lightning II disappearing into the distance.

Black smoke rose from the wreckage of downed Euro-copter. Hawk said into his comms, "That was bloody good timing."

Ilse said, "*HMS Queen Elizabeth* was sailing off the coast. Just so happens, they decided they'd help out."

"Good old Royal Navy."

"Is everyone alright down there?"

Hawk looked across at Gray and saw that he had sustained a few cuts and scratches that were bleeding. He figured he looked the same and said, "Nothing that a Band aid won't fix. All we have to do now is get to Almeria. And since Marcus killed our ride, it's going to be a frigging long walk."

Outside Almeria, Spain

"I've got him," Slania said, turning her head to look at Ilse. "He's aboard a Russian flagged ship called the *Rostov* anchored outside Almeria Port."

"Good work. How did you find him?"

"The wonders of modern technology. He's onboard with a small team of mercenaries. However, the ship itself looks to have an armed security force on it as well."

It was understandable for the *Rostov* to have its own security, with the uptick in piracy across the globe. But Ilse had a feeling that this was a little more than that. "Find out who owns it."

"On it."

Anja appeared. "Do you have something?"

Ilse told her what Slania had discovered. "That was quick."

"This is even quicker," Slania said turning. "The ship is owned by Leonid Federov."

"You are shitting me," Anja growled.

"I wish I was."

"But what does this mean?" Ilse asked.

"Let me think," Anja snapped. Her mind worked at shutter speed as she tried to process the information. Then the shutter slowed, and a picture became clear. "That bastard."

"What is it?"

"Noskov isn't in charge of Medusa, Federov is. He has been ever since Medvedev died. He had Noskov kill him."

"Why? How? He was in a secure facility," Ilse pointed out.

"I don't know, but it all fits. Noskov hasn't put a foot right since he's been in charge. So Federov gives up the hideouts so we can take him off the board and Federov will replace him with someone else."

"Jake is going to love this."

"Ilse, take that thread that Slania has just uncovered and pull it until you run it out to the end. I want to see where it leads."

"Yes, ma'am."

CHAPTER TWENTY

Almeria, Spain

THE *ROSTOV* WAS ANCHORED outside the port of Almeria waiting to sail. Its destination was Oran where it would take on a load of fertilizer which would be exported to Brazil. What wasn't known was that there was a load of arms below decks for rebels wanting to overthrow the current government in Mali.

Noskov, however, would depart in Oran to finish his journey onto Libya. But the holdup was a berth in Oran. Hence, they were still at anchor, outside the port. Besides, the captain was still drunk.

Noskov's main concern was how he had been found. There weren't many who knew about the places he'd been sequestered away in. Very few in fact. And now Federov and Peacock were uncontactable. Peacock wasn't overly troubling, but Federov was a different matter altogether.

Even though he was incarcerated, he'd always been contactable; had fed information through couriers and informants which had helped out.

But now the man who had ordered the death of Medvedev, had taken over the reins of the world's biggest trafficking operation, was silent, and it could only mean one of two things. Either they knew about him, or Noskov was now expendable and there was no further use for him.

If that were the case, Noskov needed to find the smallest hole he could find and crawl into it.

There was a knock on the bulkhead door. Noskov reached for his MP-443 Grach. He kept it behind his back and said, "Come."

The door opened and Thompson, the mercenary who'd helped him escape the underground deathtrap, entered the cabin. "What can I do for you?" Noskov asked.

"We will be sailing tomorrow afternoon."

The Russian was immediately suspicious. "Why? What is happening?"

"The captain is still drunk."

"Then find another one."

"It isn't that simple," Thompson told him.

Noskov's eyes narrowed. "Why isn't it? We're in a port, there are ship captains everywhere. Find one."

"Sir—"

"Are you defying me?"

"What?"

"It is a simple question. Are you defying me?"

"You need to calm down, mate," Thompson said becoming impatient with Federov's agitated state.

"Calm down? Me? Did you know what was going to happen at the facility? Did Boyle have a mole?"

Thompson stared at Noskov and noticed something in the man's eyes that he'd never seen there before. He was afraid. In a calm voice he said, "Sir, we'll be out of here tomorrow. Once in Oran, arrangements have been made to get you to Libya."

"Have they really? How? Have you talked to Peacock? Huh? I think you're lying. I haven't talked to him, can't even get through to him."

"We have our ways, you know that. Shit, most of the time we use your resources."

"Yes, you do." Noskov's voice had a finality about it and before Thompson could react, the Grach came up and fired twice.

The rounds punched into the mercenary's chest and made him stagger. His mouth opened and he dropped to his knees, a surprised expression on his face.

Noskov stepped closer to Thompson and looked at him as he died. "You will betray me no more."

———

IT WAS dark and the night was lit by a crescent moon. The two stealthy figures came aboard through the hawse-hole and crouched down, making sure they were clear. Once they were certain all was clear, they opened their waterproof bags and kitted up.

Hawk whispered into his comms, "Alpha, this is Bravo. We're on deck. Out."

"Copy, Bravo. Good hunting."

Hawk brought his MP5SD up to his shoulder and motioned Gray forward. He whispered into his comms, "Let's get this party started."

They began moving along the deck past the large cargo hold hatches which covered almost the entire deck. Ahead of them, Hawk could see a guard on patrol. He brought up his MP5 and put a three-round burst into him. The guard fell silently to the deck.

Hawk and Gray moved swiftly forward, dragging the downed man into the shadows. Once he was secure, they then moved around one of the large hatches towards the guard who was on the other side of the ship.

It was Gray who put this one down. A quick burst from the MP5 and the guard was dead. Again, this one was dragged into the shadows.

Using hand signals, Hawk indicated towards the bridge superstructure. Halfway up was the cabin deck. It was there they were sure that they would find Noskov.

Suddenly, Hawk's comms came to life as Anja said, "Bravo One, copy?"

"Copy," Hawk whispered.

"If you can, take the target alive."

The former SAS man glanced at his partner. "Are you serious?"

"Yes. We need him alive if possible."

Shit. "Copy. We will attempt to take the target alive."

"What the fuck is going on?" Gray asked.

"No idea. Let's just keep going."

Keeping as best they could to the shadows, the two Talon men moved forward. Ahead of them was an external ladder which led to the first deck. At the top, walking around was another guard, armed with what looked to be an AK-47.

Hawk waited in the shadows until the man turned and was going back the other way, before placing his foot on the first step. Then as silently as possible, he started to climb. He crouched down as he reached the top, taking up position where he could see through the handrail. The MP5 came up once more and as the man turned around, Hawk hit him with another short burst.

The man fell to the deck, the AK-47 clattering as it fell from his grasp. The two Talon operators waited patiently to see if anyone had been alerted by the noise. When no one appeared, they rushed forward and once more hid the body.

Gray said, "Blueprints showed that there's a door on the port side. There should be a stairwell in there which we can use to gain access to the second deck."

"Lead the way."

The two men worked their way around to the port side of the superstructure where they found the door.

Gray reached out and tried it. Hawk stood back as the door swung open, his weapon ready.

Whether it was carelessness or just plain dumb luck, there happened to be another guard standing on the other side, his hand reaching out as though he was going to open the door from inside.

Shock registered on his face as he saw the black clad man standing there. Without hesitation, Hawk squeezed the trigger and bullets punched into the guard's chest. As he fell back, his finger reflexively squeezed the trigger, and the AK-47 that he held rattled violently.

Hawk flinched as bullets ricocheted off the steel bulkheads and deck. One flew past his head, close enough for him to feel the wind of its passage. "Shit a brick," he growled.

The firing ceased as the man hit the deck, but the echoes seemed to ring throughout the ship. Gray said, "That's torn it."

"You're not frigging wrong. Up the stairs. I've got your six."

Gray stepped through the doorway and swept the passageway in front of him. He then turned left and started up the stairs. As he reached the second deck, a figure loomed large in front of him.

Whoever it was, they were unarmed, so moving on muscle memory, Gray switched around the MP5 and hammered the butt of it into the man's face. There was a sharp cry of pain before the figure collapsed at Gray's feet.

The former Para kicked the man in the head and he went still.

Gray stepped through an open doorway and started to move along the passageway. He reached an intersection which went along to his right. A shooter appeared ahead of him and the MP5 spat more bullets.

The man buckled at the knees and sank down. A sharp cry of alarm came from the passageway to his right.

He turned and saw another shooter just as the man opened fire.

Bullets ricocheted off the steel bulkheads from the AK47 as lethal rounds hammered outward from the passageway. Gray ducked back, pressing himself against the bulkhead as an intolerable hail of bullets came his way.

Behind him, he heard Hawk curse and then the former SAS man leaned around and threw an object down the passage. "Frag out!"

The sound of the explosion seemed to rock the whole ship, the blast engulfing the shooter with shrapnel.

Hawk waited a couple of heartbeats and rounded the corner. The shooter was down but another had taken his place. Hawk fired and the man jerked under the impacts of the rounds. He slumped to the deck, joining his shredded comrade.

"Contact rear!" Gray exclaimed and fired two bursts from his weapon as the shooter fired his own.

The shooter went down but Gray grunted and slumped forward. Knowing what the sound meant, Hawk stopped, and turned. Seeing his friend hunched over he said, "Are you alright?"

"Do I look all right? Gray managed. "That shit frigging hurts."

"Are you bleeding?"

"No."

"Then get up, you big Jessie."

Hawk dragged Gray to his feet. And shoved him forward. "Where the hell do we start?"

"Check on your right."

One by one they started to clear the cabins. A sailor appeared behind them. Hawk raised his weapon and said, "Go away, mate, this isn't your day."

The man turned and ran.

Suddenly a door at the end of the passageway flew

open. A figure paused, looked their way, and then disappeared. "I think that was our HVT bolting," Gray said.

"Get after him."

They started moving faster along the passageway to the end. As Gray started around it, gun fire rang out. He ducked back and took cover. "He didn't run too far."

"Who sent you?" came Noskov's voice. "Was it Federov?"

The two Talon men looked at each other. Hawk asked, "What the hell is he on about?"

"Was it? Did Federov send you?"

"Federov is locked up," Hawk called back.

"What about Peacock?"

"He's dead, I killed him. What about Federov?"

"Who are you?"

Hawk peered around the corner. Federov fired his handgun.

"Who are you? Are you Talon? Or Federov's people?"

"This bloke is frigging crazy," Hawk growled.

"Sounds like it."

"Alpha One, can we kill this tosser? He's finally cracked."

"No, I want him alive. What's he saying?" Anja asked.

"He thinks we're Federov's people. What's he on about?"

"Federov is running Medusa. I need to know how. That is why we need him alive. Understand?"

Hawk let loose a string of epithets before saying to Gray, "Looks like it's my turn to get shot."

"What?"

"I'll distract him, you shoot him," Hawk explained.

"The boss wants him alive," the former para pointed out.

"Just shoot him in the leg."

"And hope he doesn't shoot you in the head, you stupid gobshite."

246

"Let's find out."

Hawk stepped out around the corner of the passageway. Gray was right behind him. Noskov fired and Hawk twisted in pain as a bullet hit him in the ribs, left side. He felt one break and a cry of pain escaped his lips.

Meanwhile, Gray had flicked the fire selector around on the MP5 and fired a single shot. Noskov dropped to the deck as his left leg kicked out from beneath him, his handgun falling with a resounding clatter. He grabbed at the wounded appendage as he bit back the urge to cry out.

Gray hurried forward to secure the Russian. Noskov made a play for his dropped sidearm but the Brit kicked him in the leg. A howl of pain escaped his mouth and Gray rolled him over. He secured him with zip ties and dragged the Russian screeching to his feet.

"Shut the fuck up or I'll drill a bullet into your frigging head."

"You shot—oof."

The punch to the stomach traveled all of a foot but it was full of power. Noskov doubled over and retched. Gray turned to Hawk. "You all right, mucker?"

"I'll live," Hawk growled, knowing that he needed medical attention. "Let's get off this scow."

They started back along the passageway. Their path was clear but once outside, things changed. Gunfire raked the upper deck and forced them to take cover. Hawk returned the fire and saw a shooter fall. But there were at least another six to replace him. These were possibly the ship's security force.

"Damn it," Hawk snarled. "Get to the stern."

"But our equipment is at the bow," Gray pointed out. "Plus, we have a bloody prisoner to worry about."

"You will never get away," Noskov said, sounding more confident. "Surrender now."

Gray slapped him. "Once more will be the last time, shithead."

More bullets ricocheted off the bulkhead. They drew back further. "Move now, Mucker," Hawk said.

They worked their way to the stern where they looked over the rail. It was straight down to the water.

"Drop the kit and let's go," Hawk said.

"Y—you can't. I'm not going," Noskov whined.

"You're not?" Hawk asked.

"No."

The pair took a side each and threw him over. A minute or so later, they followed.

EPILOGUE

Hereford, England

"TAKE A SEAT," Anja said, pointing at a chair.

Federov grinned. "We are all together again so soon. Did you have success with your mission?"

"We did in fact."

"Good, I am pleased."

Hawk moved around behind him and suddenly the Russian became nervous. "Do you need another name from me? Is that it?"

Anja shrugged and looked at Hawk.

Suddenly Federov's face was traveling at speed towards the stainless-steel table he was seated before. There was a sickening sound as his nose flattened against the hard surface. Blood spurted and flowed onto the tabletop.

Hawk pulled the Russian's head back by his hair and spoke harshly into the stunned man's ear, "We know everything, bloke. You're the gaffer of the whole shithouse situation. The boss of it all. You had Noskov kill Medvedev and then used him as your proxy. But he was stuffing up too much and you needed him gone before word got out."

"I don't know what—what you are talking about," Federov moaned.

"You screwed up, Leonid," Anja said. "The ship that Noskov was on, was owned by you. Viktor wouldn't have made that mistake. Then, when we took Noskov alive, he confirmed everything."

"Viktor left me behind. He cared about no one but himself." The bitterness flowed out of the Russian. "But he underestimated me and my will to get revenge."

Anja nodded. "You played your part well. Giving us information which we could prove while you connived in your cell. I'm still at a loss how you did the rest of it but I'm sure it will all come out."

Hawk moved back around to stand beside Anja. He said, "But sadly your time with us has come to an end. We're handing you over to MI5. From here on out you'll be their problem."

Federov looked up at them both, his face bloody. His eyes narrowed. "You will hear of me again. I will not go quietly into the night. Do not make the same mistake Viktor made."

Hawk's voice grew savage. "I'd like to kill you, asshole, but they won't let me. Keep it up and I might just do it anyway."

Federov spat. "Go ahead, do it."

Hawk took a step toward him. "Jake, stop."

He froze, staring at the Russian with hatred. "You're lucky she's here, mate."

"You will never succeed," Federov snapped.

"We already have," said Anja. "Through that one slipup you made with the ship we've managed to find all of Medusa's foreign bank accounts. Everything has been frozen. Right now, SAS teams along with partner forces are hitting targets across the globe freeing women you have as captives ready to sell. They are also seizing weapons shipments as well. Medusa is done, Leonid. You are now boss of nothing. You thought Noskov was endangering everything, but you were the one who brought it down."

Hawk grinned. "Oops."

Federov sat there in silence, eyes darting left and right as he processed what he'd just been told. Then realization hit. It was all over. The once great criminal empire was no more. Everything would fracture and he'd be stuck in some dark hole that MI5 put him in.

By the time Anja and Hawk left the room, he was wailing like a spoilt child.

———

THEY ALL SAT around the table drinking beer. Tomorrow they would attend the memorial of a friend. The forecast was for rain, weather suitable for such a solemn occasion.

Hawk looked across the table at Slania. He pointed his bottle at her and said, "You did good, lass."

"I'm glad you approve." He wasn't sure if there was sarcasm there or not but took it good naturedly.

Anja said, "Yes, I think you will fit right in. That is if you want to stay?"

Slania nodded. "I'll stay."

"Mister Gray?"

"You'll not be able to shake me loose, boss. But there is one thing."

"What is that?"

"Who do I see about those suits? They work, but it bloody hurts when you get shot."

They all chuckled.

Anja's cell rang and she got up and moved away to answer it. Ilse was sitting next to Hawk, and he felt her

251

hand cover his under the table. He opened his to accept it and glanced at her. She smiled. "Now that Medusa is gone, what shall we do?"

"There will be fractures in the underworld that will need healing in our own special way," Hawk replied.

Slania said, "I heard that the cleanup teams have freed over four hundred sex slaves across Europe."

Ilse nodded. "Yes, but there will be those who slip through the cracks."

"We'll never be out of a job," Hawk said.

Anja disconnected the call, a look of concern on her face. "What's up, boss?" Gray asked.

"Leonid Federov was found dead in his cell twenty minutes ago."

"That'll stuff up your day," Hawk said.

"That isn't all," Anja continued, staring at the former SAS operator. "In the words of someone famous, whose porridge did you piss in?"

Hawk frowned. "Why?"

"Someone has just put a twenty-million-dollar bounty on your head. You're now a wanted man, Jake."

A LOOK AT BOOK FOUR:
TALON REPRISAL

The team everyone fears, walking a deadly line...

Someone is kidnapping young women off the street and using them for evil. When one of them is accidentally killed, the Talon team is tasked with finding out who's behind this brutal chaos. As a pattern emerges, it becomes clear that the culprit may be someone they least suspect.

Soon, the team is drawn deep into a web of deceit and are—once again—fighting for their very lives and those they want to protect.

At the the end of it all, will an unforeseen twist shock them beyond repair?

AVAILABLE JANUARY 2023

ABOUT THE AUTHOR

A relative newcomer to the world of writing, Brent Towns self-published his first book, a western, in 2015. *Last Stand in Sanctuary* took him two years to write. His first hardcover book, a Black Horse Western, was published the following year.

Since then, he has written 26 western stories, including some in collaboration with British western author, Ben Bridges.

Also, he has written the novelization to the upcoming 2019 movie from One-Eyed Horse Productions, titled, *Bill Tilghman and the Outlaws*. Not bad for an Australian author, he thinks.

Brent Towns has also scripted three Commando Comics with another two to come.

He says, "The obvious next step for me was to venture into the world of men's action/adventure/thriller stories. Thus, Team Reaper was born."

A country town in Queensland, Australia, is where Brent lives with his wife and son.

In the past, he worked as a seaweed factory worker, a knife-hand in an abattoir, mowed lawns and tidied gardens, worked in caravan parks, and worked in the hire industry. And now, as well as writing books, Brent is a home tutor for his son doing distance education.

Brent's love of reading used to take over his life, now it's writing that does that; often sitting up until the small hours, bashing away at his tortured keyboard where he loses himself in the world of fiction.